MYSTERY AT THE CROSSROADS

Books by

CAROLYN KEENE

Nancy Drew Mystery Stories

The Secret of the Old Clock
The Hidden Staircase
The Bungalow Mystery
The Mystery at Lilac Inn
The Secret at Shadow Ranch
The Secret of Red Gate Farm
The Clue in the Diary
Nancy's Mysterious Letter
The Sign of the Twisted Candles
The Password to Larkspur Lane
The Clue of the Broken Locket
The Message in the Hollow Oak
The Mystery of the Ivory Charm
The Whispering Statue
The Haunted Bridge
The Clue of the Tapping Heels

The Mystery of the Brass Bound Trunk
The Mystery at the Moss-Covered Mansion
The Quest of the Missing Map
The Clue in the Jewel Box
The Secret in the Old Attic
The Clue in the Crumbling Wall
The Mystery of the Tolling Bell
The Clue in the Old Album
The Ghost of Blackwood Hall
The Clue of the Leaning Chimney
The Secret of the Wooden Lady
The Clue of the Black Keys
The Mystery at the Ski Jump
The Clue of the Velvet Mask

The Ringmaster's Secret

Dana Girls Mystery Stories

By the Light of the Study Lamp
The Secret at Lone Tree Cottage
In the Shadow of the Tower
A Three-Cornered Mystery
The Secret at the Hermitage
The Circle of Footprints
The Mystery of the Locked Room
The Clue in the Cobweb

The Secret at the Gatehouse
The Mysterious Fireplace
The Clue of the Rusty Key
The Portrait in the Sand
The Secret in the Old Well
The Clue in the Ivy
The Secret of the Jade Ring
Mystery at the Crossroads

"What have you done with my daughter?" Sando demanded.

The DANA GIRLS *Mystery Stories*

MYSTERY AT THE CROSSROADS

By

CAROLYN KEENE

Grosset & Dunlap, *Publishers*
NEW YORK

Contents

MYSTERY AT THE CROSSROADS

CHAPTER I

The Mysterious Cry

"WE'RE lost, Jean!"

"Sh, Doris! Don't let Professor Crandall hear you." Blond, vivacious Jean Dana turned to the girl beside her on the rear seat of the Starhurst School station wagon. "You'll hurt his feelings."

Jean nodded toward the driver. Beside him was Jean's elder sister, dark-haired, serious-minded Louise. Doris Harland, who did not relish the thought of being lost in this deserted wooded area, was seated between Jean Dana and Evelyn Starr. The Starr family had once owned the extensive estate which was now the site of the well-known boarding school.

Louise turned and smiled knowingly at the girls in the rear seat. Professor Crandall, though loved by all the Starhurst students, was known to be the most absent-minded man in Penfield. Today, a cloudy afternoon in May, he seemed more abstracted than usual.

"I think I know where we are," Evelyn spoke up. "And the sooner we get away from here, the better I'll like it!"

"Why?" Jean asked.

"Because this area is—well, haunted. There's an old abandoned inn over there—with a ghost, people say!" Evelyn pointed to the woods, which appeared gloomy in spite of the spring foliage.

Jean chuckled. "The ghost you told us about?"

Evelyn nodded. She had once related to a group of students the story about a summer hotel of the Civil War era which had been abandoned many years before. Queer happenings in connection with the ghost were reported from time to time.

"Does anybody believe those stories?" Jean asked incredulously, though her eyes sparkled with lively interest.

Evelyn shrugged. "I know everyone avoids this spot—even for picnics."

Doris was becoming more nervous by the moment. She tapped Professor Crandall on the shoulder. "Please, can't we speed up a little?" she pleaded.

"Er—why, yes." The professor abruptly came out of his reverie. "Are we late?" he asked, glancing at the dashboard clock. As he gave the motor an extra spurt of speed, he remarked, "Let's see. Did Starhurst win the tennis tournament today?"

The girls stifled giggles. Professor Crandall had

accompanied them on an all-day jaunt to Ashton School, where the four Starhurst girls in the car had won a victory from their opponents. But he had spent the entire time in the school's library and now was not even sure which school had won.

"Why, we won, of course," Evelyn told him, and added wistfully, "There was to be a big celebration at Starhurst at five o'clock, but we're too late now for that."

"I'm sorry," the professor murmured. "My new lecture is constantly on my mind—" His voice trailed off and he did not explain further.

"Oh!" Doris cried suddenly.

"What's the matter?" the other girls chorused.

Doris declared that she had seen a man peering at them from among the trees. "He—he was wild-look-ing!"

Jean laughed and remarked, "You're trying hard to give us the creeps, Doris."

"And pretty soon you'll succeed," Louise said, smiling. There was silence in the car for nearly five minutes as each girl peered anxiously ahead for familiar landmarks. Suddenly Louise cried, "Look out, Professor Crandall!"

He jammed on the brakes and the car screeched to a halt at a crossroads just in time to miss a sedan which shot from the bisecting road.

Louise was the first one to recover from their fright.

"A gypsy is driving that car!" she exclaimed.

The lone occupant had a yellow scarf wrapped around his head and large golden rings dangled from his ears.

"He may be a gypsy, but he's also a speed demon," Jean declared angrily. She turned to Evelyn. "Is there a band of gypsies around here?"

"I never heard of one," Evelyn replied. "But this territory would just suit them. Say, you don't suppose that ghost at the old inn could be a gypsy, do you?"

"I wonder," Jean mused.

"Let's go," Doris begged Professor Crandall again. She was more apprehensive than ever.

Stunned by the near accident, the professor had been sitting immobile. Now he shook himself and drove on. Louise glanced at him wondering why the prospect of his forthcoming lecture would cause him to be more absent-minded than usual.

"We'd better get to Starhurst soon," Evelyn whispered, "or Mrs. Crandall may take away our privileges for a while."

The professor's wife, headmistress of Starhurst School, was a stern disciplinarian. Her students were slightly in awe of her and the reprimands which followed infringements of the rules.

"We can't be blamed for being late this time," Jean reassured Evelyn with an impish grin.

A quarter of a mile farther on, Professor Crandall

stopped. Then he started to back the car around.

"I believe we should have taken that other road," he said.

Louise leaned out the window to watch the deep roadside ditch. In case the professor got too close to it, she would warn him.

Suddenly she heard a strange sound. From somewhere in the woods came a mournful wailing. Louise asked Professor Crandall to stop. In a few seconds the wailing was followed by a young woman's voice singing a plaintive song in a foreign tongue. The melody ended abruptly. There was a prolonged, heartbreaking cry, a scream, then silence.

Without a moment's hesitation Louise jumped from the car. "We must help her!" she declared and rushed into the woods.

"But, girls . . ." Professor Crandall began, as the others followed her. Then, resignedly, he said, "Well, be careful, now, and hurry back. I'll meet you at the crossroads."

The group caught up to Louise and plowed through the tangled undergrowth. There was no sign of the person who had cried out.

"Let's call," Louise suggested. Cupping her hands to her mouth, she cried out, "Hello! Anyone here?"

Silence. The other girls called out but received no answer—only the echo of their voices floating eerily back.

"Let's go back to the car," Doris urged. "I don't like this place. And we might be near the old inn with the ghost."

"But if someone's been hurt, we've got to help her," Louise insisted.

Against her better judgment, Doris trailed along. Suddenly the girls came to a clearing. Louise, who was in the lead, stopped and pointed.

Ahead loomed a large dilapidated structure. The old Civil War inn! Dry leaves skittered across a wide front veranda, lodging here and there in rotted holes in the flooring. Dirty gray paint was blistered and peeling. The whole place seemed desolate and forbidding.

"O-oh, it's creepy!" whispered Doris.

"Do you think the person we heard wailing could be inside?" Evelyn asked in a low voice.

Without answering, Louise and Jean started up the rickety steps. Doris grabbed their arms.

"Don't go in! It's too dangerous!" she said. "You might fall through the floor and break your necks."

The Danas paused a moment to look at the boarded-up windows. There was some merit to their friend's advice, and Evelyn decided to heed it. She added her plea that the sisters were running an unnecessary risk of being injured.

"But if someone needs our help—" Louise began.

"We'll watch our step," Jean promised.

While Doris and Evelyn looked on, worried, Louise and Jean gingerly crossed the porch and tried the front door. Upon finding it locked, they pulled at a board over the nearest window. It came off easily and revealed one small, paneless sash. Louise slipped her hand through, turned the catch, and raised the window. The sill was black with grime, but the sisters climbed over it, unmindful of their pastel sports skirts and jackets.

They stepped into the gloomy interior, testing the floor before proceeding further. Dust swirled up about their feet and cobwebs clung to their faces and hands.

"This must have been the lobby," Jean said, observing a clerk's desk opposite the entrance. Her words sounded unnaturally loud in the deep stillness.

"And what a grand old staircase!" Louise added, brushing at the persistent cobwebs. "It looks so—"

Her words were choked off in a gasp as she caught sight of a shadowy figure flitting up the steps!

CHAPTER II

A Strange Find

"Did—did you see what I saw, Louise?" Jean gasped, dashing to the staircase.

"The ghost? It looked pretty real to me. Yes, I'm sure I saw someone go up those stairs," Louise whispered.

As she followed, the floor groaned and once she stepped into a wide crack. Jean, part way up the staircase, called:

"Hello, hello! Anyone up there who needs help?"

Louise joined her and their shouts echoed weirdly throughout the inn.

There was no answer.

"Whoever it was apparently doesn't want our help," Jean declared as they reached the second story. "Shall we look any more?"

Louise did not reply, but started walking carefully

8

through the dark, musty hallway. The floor sagged and creaked under her, and twice the decayed boards gave way. Finally she stopped.

"I think we've done as much as we dare," she said. "This place is dangerous to investigate without a light. We might be seriously hurt."

"Probably that sad singing and cry for help came from outdoors, anyway," Jean concluded. "Let's look around the grounds."

The girls retraced their steps to the first floor, but by this time their curiosity about the old inn was thoroughly aroused.

"This place can't be far from Penfield," Jean commented. "Let's come back here soon and really explore it."

"That's a good idea. And next time we'll be sure to bring flashlights!"

"Yes!" exclaimed Jean, disappointed not to have found out anything about the mysterious figure.

When they reached the porch, the Danas were surprised not to find Evelyn and Doris waiting for them. Louise was a little worried, but Jean decided that their friends had walked to the car. Again Louise and Jean called out that they would help anyone in trouble but received no answer.

"We'd better leave," Louise said.

Both girls had inquiring minds but they were always quick to help anyone in distress.

Because of this willingness to think first of others, Louise and Jean were the most popular students at Starhurst School, much to the envy of the school's troublemaker, Lettie Briggs. But the Danas' friends were proud of the sisters' school records, their athletic ability, and especially of their success in solving mysteries.

Only a short while before, the Danas had brought favorable publicity to Starhurst School by recovering a valuable heirloom that had been stolen. Their adventures in connection with *The Secret of the Jade Ring* had been the most exciting they had ever encountered.

When not in school, the girls lived in Oak Falls with a maiden aunt, Miss Harriet Dana, and her brother, the girls' Uncle Ned, captain of the steamship *Balaska*. Cora Appel, a kindly but awkward maid of all work, completed the little household.

As Louise and Jean made their way to the road, they met Doris and Evelyn, who had been looking around also. They, too, had seen no one.

When Jean told them about the flitting figure, Doris shivered a bit. "I'm glad you didn't stay. Come on!" she urged. "We've kept Professor Crandall waiting a long time."

"Yes, we must hurry," Louise agreed.

Walking rapidly, the four students started through the woodland toward the road. They had not gone far when Jean suddenly stopped. Her gaze had been drawn to a dark metal object half buried in the soft earth. Curious, she prodded it with the toe of her shoe.

"Why, it's a spoon!" she exclaimed. "An odd one, too."

Jean picked up the spoon and rubbed it free of dirt. The spoon, made of fine-quality silver, was ornate and the end of the handle was carved in the form of a man's head with long hair and a beard.

"This must be an antique!" Evelyn remarked. "You've made a real find, Jean."

"How do you suppose such a spoon happened to be here?" Jean speculated. "It must have been dropped recently, or it would have been completely covered over."

She put it into her jacket pocket and the four girls hastened on. It took them longer than they had expected to reach the crossroads. To their dismay, the school car was not there!

"Now what's become of Professor Crandall?" Evelyn fretted. "He's so absent-minded, it's nerve-racking."

Louise and Jean glanced at each other. They sincerely hoped that only absent-mindedness was the answer. But suppose the professor had been accosted and the car stolen! The Danas tacitly decided not to express their fears.

"He turned in this direction," Louise said, noting

the tire tracks. She forced a laugh. "We may find him parked around the next bend, reading a book."

The girls trudged to the first bend in the road. But Professor Crandall was not there.

"We're really stuck!" Doris gasped. "Now what will we do?"

"Walk," Louise said cheerfully. "Evelyn, do you think this may be the direction to Penfield?"

"I think it is. Anyway, we can inquire. I'm sure we'll meet a car soon or find a house."

It was growing dark and Doris eyed the tall bushes with misgiving. But deciding that there was safety in numbers, her fears subsided somewhat.

"Here comes a car now," said Louise, whose keen ears had picked up the hum of a motor far down the road. "Traveling fast, too."

Moving aside, the girls prepared to hail the driver. But as the car came into view, they realized it would be useless. The long, sleek sedan shot past them at great speed, throwing up a cloud of dust.

"Another gypsy!" Jean exclaimed as she caught a glimpse of a man with dark skin and shaggy hair. He wore large earrings as the first gypsy had, but he was considerably older.

"There must be a camp of them nearby!" Evelyn exclaimed with conviction.

"All the more reason for us to move along," announced Doris, starting hurriedly on.

"Those gypsies may be only passing through here," said Louise. "That was an out-of-state license."

Nevertheless, all the girls were nervous as they trudged along.

"I'm so provoked at Professor Crandall!" Evelyn said. "Whatever became of him?"

Quarter of a mile's walk brought the girls to a paved road. At Evelyn's suggestion they turned right and presently came to a gasoline station. A friendly attendant set their fears at rest by telling them that they were not far from Penfield.

Louise thanked him and asked if he had noticed a station wagon with a gray-haired gentleman in it within the last half-hour.

"Did he wear glasses?"

"Yes. That would be Professor Crandall!"

"He stopped at my station to ask how to get to Penfield."

Louise heaved a sigh of relief, then chuckled. "We were afraid maybe he'd been injured."

"By those gypsies we saw!" Doris added. "They don't know how to drive!"

"Those gypsies!" exclaimed the station attendant with a shake of his head.

"Do they have a camp near here?" Louise asked quickly.

"I suspect so. I've seen their cars whizzing past. But they never buy any gasoline here."

Thanking the attendant again, the girls walked on. Finally, they came within view of the western outskirts of Penfield.

"Thank goodness!" exclaimed Doris. "My feet are killing me!"

Jean had noted an approaching automobile. "Isn't that the school car?" she asked hopefully.

"It is!" Evelyn decided a moment later. "Professor Crandall must be coming back!"

He pulled up beside the girls. "Well, well, so here you are," the professor greeted them. "I hope you didn't have too long a walk."

The girls climbed in, almost too weary to reply, but finally Evelyn asked, "Why did you go off without us?"

The professor chuckled. "It seems as if when I remember to do one thing, I forget another. Mrs. Crandall asked me to stop in the country and buy some eggs. While I was waiting for you, I suddenly recalled the errand."

Jean did not notice any package in the car. "Did you get the eggs?" she asked.

The professor shook his head. "When I got to the farm I couldn't recall how many dozen I was supposed to buy. Mrs. Crandall wrote it down, but I seem to have mislaid the paper."

The girls grinned and began to suggest various amounts. He shook his head.

"We're big eaters," Jean said finally with a chuckle. "Was it twenty dozen perhaps?"

"I don't recall—"

"Twenty-four?"

"Ah, that was it!" cried the professor. "We'll have to stop in town for them."

His mind relieved, he drove hurriedly into Penfield. Louise began to tell him of their adventure at the old inn but he did not seem to be listening. From his responses she was certain that he heard only half of what she was saying.

Professor Crandall parked in front of a delicatessen on Main Street. The girls waited in the car while he went inside.

"The poor dear's been especially forgetful today," Louise commented. "He must be worrying about something besides the lecture."

"He usually is," Doris said, laughing.

"I hope he doesn't forget that we're waiting," Evelyn said. "I'm starved and it's nearly dinnertime."

Jean had been looking at a jewelry store next door to the delicatessen. The proprietor was just closing up.

"While we're waiting, I'm going to run in there and show the jeweler this silver spoon I found at the inn," she decided impulsively. "He might be able to tell me something of its history."

The other girls trailed her into the shop. Mr. Claude, the proprietor, paused in the act of drawing the venetian blind to talk to Jean. As he examined the spoon, his eager expression showed that he was deeply interested.

"May I inquire how you obtained this?" he asked.

Jean replied that she had found it not far from Penfield. "Is it old?"

"Definitely. The spoon appears to be medieval silver."

"Jean, you're in luck!" cried Evelyn.

Mr. Claude looked at her intently. "That depends entirely upon one's point of view," was his surprising comment. "A collector would treasure such a spoon as this. As for myself, I'm not sure I'd want to own it."

The girls were puzzled by the jeweler's strange remark.

"What do you mean?" Jean asked quickly.

"Are you superstitious?" he asked, eying her appraisingly.

"I never thought so." Jean gave her sister a puzzled glance.

"Well, that's fortunate," Mr. Claude replied. "Perhaps I shouldn't tell you this, but I feel it's my duty to warn you."

"Warn us?" Jean echoed. "What do you mean?"

"According to legend, this spoon has a curse on it," the jeweler said gravely. "It may bring you very bad luck!"

ưư

CHAPTER III

Hunting a Ghost

The jeweler's astounding remark about the silver spoon bringing bad luck to Jean Dana made Doris and Evelyn wince. But Louise's and Jean's eyes glistened in anticipation of another mystery.

Had the person they had heard singing in the woods lost the spoon? Had she cried out because someone had tried to take it from her? Jean begged Mr. Claude for more information.

"I'll show you a picture," he replied.

Disappearing into an inner office, the jeweler reappeared a moment later with a heavy leather-bound volume. Thumbing through it, he came to a colored plate which showed reproductions of several fine antique spoons.

"Why, this looks exactly like the one I found!" Jean asserted as she peered at the picture.

"Yes, and read what it says beneath it," Mr. Claude

17

said. "According to this, a cruel Middle East king many centuries ago sent a silver spoon as a gift to an enemy whom he suspected of plotting to seize his throne. Everyone who used the spoon died."

"But that's only a story, isn't it?" Evelyn asked nervously.

"Supposedly a true one. The silver, you see, was impregnated with poison."

Doris gasped. "Oh, Jean, you must get rid of it immediately!"

"Not on your life! It's too beautiful. Besides," Jean added, "I can't believe even a poisoned spoon would be dangerous after all these years."

"Probably not," the jeweler agreed. "Nevertheless, if I were you, I wouldn't put that spoon to practical use."

"Don't worry. I won't eat with it," Jean promised. "I'll keep it as a souvenir."

"And what a souvenir!" Mr. Claude sighed. "Odd that a spoon like that should turn up here in Penfield. I've never seen one." Then he added, "Don't put too much stock in that legend. I'm sure the curse, like the poison, has lost most of its power by now."

Jean thanked the jeweler and the girls went back to the car. Just then Professor Crandall came from the delicatessen, carrying a crate filled with boxes of eggs.

Jean started to relate what she had learned about the spoon, but his lack of attentiveness discouraged her.

"Nice—very nice," he kept murmuring, as he drove toward Starhurst School. She gave up, and resumed discussing the medieval piece with the others.

A short time later the station wagon turned into the winding road which led to the school. The girls always felt a thrill of pride and home-coming when approaching Starhurst.

The former Starr mansion, though used for dormitory and classrooms, had lost none of its beauty and grandeur. The stately colonial building was surrounded by vast stretches of lawn and tall trees.

Now, as the professor stopped the car at the main entrance, Louise exclaimed, "Gracious! Only twenty minutes before the dinner bell!" She grabbed her tennis racket and jumped from the car.

Jean followed her quickly to their small suite on the second floor. The outer room, cheerful and cozily furnished in light walnut and flowered chintz, was used as a study. Adjoining this was the sisters' bedroom.

After hurriedly changing their clothes, the Danas went down the wide, graceful stairway with its carved balustrade. Below, in the spacious reception hall, many of the girls had gathered. The Danas joined a group of friends to whom Jean was soon proudly displaying the silver spoon.

As the girls were admiring it, Lettie Briggs sauntered in with her roommate, Ina Mason. Ina was almost as heartily disliked by their classmates as her chum. Lettie, the only daughter of a wealthy business-man, bored everyone by constantly boasting about her high social position. Ina, her shadow, was known as a bearer of tales, usually false ones.

"Where did you get that spoon, Jean?" Lettie demanded, noticing it instantly.

"Oh, that's a mystery," Jean answered airily.

"Humph! The silver is badly tarnished," Lettie said, peering closely at the odd design. "You picked it up at a junk store, I'll bet!"

"That just proves you don't recognize a genuine antique when you see one," Evelyn spoke up. "There's not another spoon like it in Penfield. Don't get too close, though."

"What do you mean?" Lettie demanded, going for the bait. "Will it explode?"

"The spoon is dangerous—very dangerous," Jean informed her soberly, suppressing a grin.

"Jean, don't forget to wash your hands carefully after handling it," added Louise, to further mystify Lettie and Ina.

"Let me see that spoon," Lettie ordered, snatching it.

"Oh, oh! Now you've done it!" Jean exclaimed in mock horror. "The poison—"

Lettie dropped the spoon on the floor. "Poison?" she faltered.

"This antique is a very rare one, used by an old king to kill off his enemies," Doris informed her. "According to the story, the metal was impregnated with a deadly poison."

"And you let me touch it!" Lettie shuddered. "For goodness' sake, do something!"

"Perhaps we can save you," Jean said, still keeping her expression very solemn.

To the merriment of the students, she waved her hands over the girl's head and muttered a few strange syllables that sounded convincingly like a witch's incantation. The other girls howled with laughter. Only then did Lettie realize that she had been made the butt of a joke.

"Think you're funny, don't you, Jean Dana?" she snapped. "Just wait!"

"Seriously, Lettie, if I were you, I would wash my hands after handling that spoon," Louise advised gravely.

"When I want your advice, I'll ask for it!" Lettie retorted rudely. "Come on, Ina!"

Linking arms with her only friend, Lettie stalked toward the dining room. Eyes flashing, she confided to her sympathetic chum:

"I'll get even with Jean and Louise if it's the last thing I do!"

"How?"

Lettie confessed that at the moment she did not have

a plan. "But I'll think of something! They're not smart enough to keep secrets from me. I'll soon find out where they got the spoon."

That night at dinner both Lettie and Ina slyly asked questions of Evelyn and Doris. Neither girl would reveal where Jean had found the silver spoon. Their teasing silence angered Lettie even more.

After dinner Jean showed the spoon to Miss Parker, a young history teacher interested in antiques.

"It's remarkable!" Miss Parker exclaimed. "Where did you find such a rare piece?"

Jean glanced carefully about to make certain that neither Ina nor Lettie was within hearing distance, then told Miss Parker of the brief visit to the old inn.

"Since coming to Starhurst this year I've heard rumors about that historical landmark," the teacher replied. "I'd love to see the place."

Jean was quick to seize this possible opportunity of returning to the crossroads area.

"Perhaps if you speak to Mrs. Crandall about it, she will give Louise and me permission to take you there," she suggested.

"A splendid idea! I'm sure that can be arranged. Will you girls be free tomorrow after classes?"

"Yes. After three o'clock."

"Fine!" Miss Parker said enthusiastically. "I'll see Mrs. Crandall at once and ask her if we may use one of the school cars."

The teacher readily arranged for the trip. Jean and Louise were careful not to mention their plans to anyone except Evelyn and Doris.

En route to the crossroads, Miss Parker told Louise and Jean that a visitor who was coming to the school might be interested in the spoon. He was Professor John Stanley, a noted authority on the influence of Europe on various phases of American history.

"He's to deliver a lecture this evening," the teacher added. "Mrs. Crandall says his letter of reference was most impressive."

"I'd like to hear him," Louise remarked.

Jean said, "I don't mean to change the subject, but isn't the air wonderful? Everything smells so fresh and—and *green!*"

Louise and Miss Parker laughingly agreed that Jean's description was perfect.

When they arrived at the crossroads, Louise suggested that they park there and walk to the inn.

"If we don't let that ghost know we're coming, maybe we can get a better look at it," she said.

Miss Parker laughed as she locked the ignition and removed the key. To it was attached a large school identification tag which would not fit into her small purse. She handed the key to Louise.

"You have a deep pocket in your dress," she observed. "Suppose you carry the key."

The three walked toward the old inn, ducking

under low-hanging limbs and pausing to admire a profusion of spring wild flowers.

"Oh, aren't they lovely!" Jean exclaimed.

"Let's pick some on our way back," Louise suggested. "We can arrange them in those twin Bavarian vases Uncle Ned sent us. They'll look scrumptious on our desks."

"Then I'll never finish that English literature book report!" Jean laughed.

"Oh, look!" Miss Parker cried. "A lilac bush! And this looks as if it were once a huge bed of tulips. The grounds around this old hotel must have been perfectly beautiful at one time. What a shame—"

Suddenly Jean gasped. "Listen! I hear that same wailing sound!"

"And it's certainly coming from the direction of the inn," Louise said excitedly. "This time we may learn what's going on around here!"

Moving carefully in order not to make a sound, the Dana girls led the way through the woods.

"A woman *must* be inside the inn," Jean whispered as the trio halted at the clearing's edge. "Hear her singing?"

Louise and Miss Parker nodded. The voice was definitely coming from the inn.

"She's very sad," the teacher observed. "I wonder—"

Miss Parker stopped speaking because the singing ceased abruptly and was followed by a scream.

Suddenly a man's voice was raised in harsh command:

"Get out of here and stay out!"

From a rear door of the inn rushed a young gypsy girl, obviously terrified. Gathering her full skirt of orange and scarlet, she raced for the shelter of the woods.

CHAPTER IV

Nura's Troubles

"I'LL bet she's the 'ghost'!" cried Jean as the gypsy girl fled among the trees.

"A very live and pretty one, too," Miss Parker commented.

"Let's try to find out what's wrong," Louise urged. "And why that man ordered her out of the inn. Come on!"

They started in pursuit. Darting along the trail the fleet-footed gypsy had taken, they soon caught sight of a bright orange-and-scarlet skirt. The girl was walking now with a fast, easy gait.

"Wait!" Jean called. "We're friends."

The gypsy girl turned quickly. Her sleek, black hair hung in two braids, plaited with old gold coins and bits of colored silk. The long, full skirt swung gracefully about her ankles.

26

"Please wait and talk to us," Louise urged as the girl seemed to hesitate. "Perhaps we can help you."

"Gypsies want no help from *gajos*," the stranger replied. But her voice was shy and she did not run away as Jean and Louise approached closer with the teacher.

"Gajos?" Jean asked, puzzled.

"A gajo is anyone who is not a gypsy, Jean," Miss Parker replied.

The sisters nodded.

"Who ordered you from the inn?" Louise asked indignantly.

The gypsy girl's dark eyes flashed. "A policeman! He came at me with a big club. I had to run, but I will go back to my home later."

"You mean the old inn is your home?" Jean questioned, astonished. "You live there?"

The gypsy girl stared hard at the Danas. Then her expression became sad. "One cannot always choose," she answered, "when one has little money."

"You are staying here alone?" Jean asked.

The girl smiled. "A gypsy is never alone when there are trees and birds and lovely sunsets," she answered evasively. "But I'm afraid when I sing now, my song is always a lament." The others knew that it was her way of telling them she was not with her people.

"Won't you tell us your name?" Louise requested kindly, trying to break through the wall of shyness.

"Nura."

"That's a pretty name. Are you a Romany gypsy?"

Nura smiled and nodded. "I may not be a gypsy long," she confided suddenly. "My *dado*—my father, that is, has ordered me to marry Zarko, a man of our tribe. But Zarko is mean and cruel! If I become his wife he will make me tell fortunes all day and he will keep my earnings. I will never marry him—never! Besides," she added shyly, "I love Stivo. I just couldn't give him up. He's—" The gypsy girl stopped suddenly as if she had felt that she had confided too much.

"Tell us about Stivo," Louise urged.

Nura's brown eyes became soft as velvet, her shyness forgotten. "Ah, he is wonderful—so strong and brave and kind! But—but Stivo has been banished from our tribe."

"Oh," said Louise, "that's too bad."

She was deeply stirred by the girl's story. But she had read that gypsies sometimes make up tales merely to conceal true facts about themselves.

"It was by order of Sando, king of the gypsies," Nura went on. Then she added quietly, "The king is my father."

"We would like to help you, Nura," Louise said in sympathy.

"How can you help me?" the gypsy girl shrugged. "Sando will take no advice from a gajo."

"If you are in the right, there must be some way to make your father see your point of view," Jean insisted. "Why does he dislike your sweetheart Stivo?"

"Because Stivo has no money. But Zarko offered one thousand dollars and a car for me," Nura answered scornfully. "He would buy me as he trades his horses!"

Miss Parker had listened attentively to the gypsy girl's words. "But isn't it customary for a gypsy to purchase his bride?" she asked.

"It is a custom which is being followed less and less in our tribe."

"Was there no other reason why your father turned down Stivo's proposal?"

Nura now avoided the teacher's direct gaze. Ill at ease, she scuffed the toe of her shoe in the dirt. "There was another reason," she admitted reluctantly. "Stivo was accused of stealing a fine old *skafidi*."

"A skafidi?" Louise asked.

"A large silver tray. It disappeared from one of the tents. Then some tribal jewelry brought from England was taken. But Stivo had nothing to do with it! My father had no right to accuse and banish him."

Nura's eyes blazed as she continued. "After that, I ran away so I would not have to marry that fat, ugly Zarko. As soon as Stivo makes a little money, he will come for me. Then we will marry."

"And always live away from your people?" Miss Parker inquired softly.

"It makes me very sad to think of it," Nura admitted. "A Romany separated from her family and tribe can be very lonely. But I will never give up Stivo."

The gypsy girl smiled slightly as she concluded her story. "So the old inn is now my home," she said.

Before anyone could comment, an automobile horn sounded. The loud honking plainly came from the nearby roadway.

"That sounds like the horn of our car!" Miss Parker exclaimed. "What could have happened?"

The teacher ran off in the direction of the road. Jean quickly caught up with her. It was only when they reached the roadside that they realized Louise had not followed them. But they assumed she had lingered behind, so that Nura would not run away again.

The station wagon stood where it had been parked. No one was around, but Jean noticed that the front left-hand door was slightly ajar. She pointed this out and said:

"Look, someone *was* honking the horn!"

"But why?" asked the teacher, nervously. "I should have locked the doors of the car, too. Oh, dear!" She stood lost in thought for a moment. "Perhaps someone wanted to summon us, Jean, but why did he leave?"

Jean did not reply. But she felt sure that the honking had been a ruse to get the visitors out of the woods.

As she was studying the dusty road for footprints, a shrill scream came from among the trees.

"Oh, goodness!" Miss Parker cried. "Now what has happened? I hope Louise—"

Jean had already started to run in the direction of the sound, and the teacher was close on her heels.

"That gypsy girl may have attacked Louise!" she said fearfully. "Nura seemed innocent enough, but I didn't entirely believe her story."

Jean was the first to reach the place where they had left her sister and the pretty gypsy.

Both had disappeared!

"Oh, this is dreadful," Miss Parker cried. "I feel responsible for the safety of you girls."

"Please, Miss Parker, don't worry," Jean said. "I'm sure we'll find them soon."

"But, Jean, we aren't familiar with these woods. How can we search the whole area?"

"I don't think that will be necessary," Jean replied. She knew that Louise and Nura could not have gone far in the short time she and Miss Parker had been away.

The two stood still, trying to decide what to do, when another cry from a different direction rang through the trees. It sent chills down the spines of Jean and her companion.

"Do you think those screams were made by the same person?" the teacher asked.

Jean, more puzzled than ever, and extremely worried about her sister, did not reply.

Once more they struggled through the underbrush, trying to trace the source of the scream. They were very near the old inn when they again heard the wild cry. This time it had come from deep in the woods. Jean was convinced, now, that the cries were being made to confuse them. She had never been more non-plused or worried in her life.

"We're losing ground," Miss Parker gasped.

Winded, she halted a moment to regain her breath and think what to do. Suddenly the car horn started honking again. The sound unnerved the teacher, who cried:

"It's—it's like chasing a phantom!"

CHAPTER V

"Follow Me!"

"Ghosts! Phantoms! I can see why people say this place is haunted!" Miss Parker exclaimed. "Jean, we *must* rescue Louise!"

Jean did not move. She was not going to be misled again. Sure that someone was trying to get her away from the immediate vicinity, she determined not to leave it.

"If Louise is here, Miss Parker," Jean stated, "I believe she's close by. Let's look."

In hurried whispers she explained her idea. Her conclusions alarmed Miss Parker even more.

"Maybe we should find that policeman and get him to help us," she said falteringly.

But instantly the teacher realized that was impractical. If he were still at the spot, he would already be busy trying to find the person who had screamed. This

33

thought gave her hope that Louise might have been saved from harm by the officer.

Jean had no such optimistic outlook. She was convinced that her sister, as well as Nura, were in danger. She must locate them at once! She began calling Louise's name, but there was no reply.

"Let's go back to the spot where we left Louise," Jean suggested and hurried toward it, followed by Miss Parker.

From there Jean followed the trampled undergrowth, repeatedly calling out, "Louise!"

"We've lost the trail completely, I'm afraid," the teacher said, as she noticed that the grass and weeds about them looked undisturbed. "Jean, I'm frightened! We never should have left Louise alone with the gypsy girl."

"I can't believe that Nura harmed her. Something else must have happened."

"But what, Jean? Where are they?"

"I'm going to walk in a wide circle to see if I can pick up their trail," Jean replied with determination.

They went on, pushing aside the thorny bushes which tore at their clothing. Suddenly Jean paused, and her heart began to pound. Through the trees she saw someone lying on the ground!

Louise!

With a cry of alarm, Jean dashed ahead to her

sister's side. Louise lay very still, but to Jean's relief she was only unconscious.

As Jean lifted her sister's head, Louise's lips moved slightly and she moaned. Jean noticed then that there was a slight swelling on her forehead above the left temple. The skin had been broken, but fortunately the cut was a small one.

By this time Miss Parker had caught up to Jean.

"Oh, thank goodness, you've found Louise. Is she badly injured?" she asked, kneeling beside the limp form.

"I don't think so. She was knocked out. She's start-ing to regain consciousness now. If only we had some water—"

"I'll try to get some. I noticed a brook, but I don't have anything to carry water—"

"Wait!" Jean interrupted. "It may not be necessary. She's stirring."

Even as she spoke, her sister's eyes opened. For several seconds Louise lay perfectly still, staring blankly into Jean's face. Then she managed a faint smile.

"She'll be all right," Miss Parker sighed in relief. "I guess she was only stunned."

Gradually, Louise pulled herself together. Some minutes passed, however, before she could tell what had happened.

"Where is Nura?" were her first words.

"That's what we'd like to know," Miss Parker replied a bit grimly. "Did she attack you after we left?"

"Oh, no!"

"Then what did happen?"

"We heard a scream and started to investigate. Nura was ahead of me—she runs like a young deer. Something dark sailed through the air and hit my head and—well, that's the last I remember."

"Nura didn't come back to help you?"

"She probably didn't know that I was hurt. She was running a good distance in front of me."

"The girl has vanished at any rate," said Miss Parker. "And I'm not in favor of looking for her. We must get back to Starhurst School at once."

"Without finding out what became of Nura?" Louise asked in disappointment.

"And I'd like to find whatever it was that hit your head, Louise," Jean added.

"That will have to wait until another day," Miss Parker insisted. "Perhaps you should have that wound on your head dressed."

"Oh, it's nothing—a mere scratch," Louise assured her. "My head throbs a bit, but that's to be expected."

Jean and Louise were reluctant to leave without learning where Nura had gone. But they felt that the gypsy girl probably was able to take care of herself.

"Can you walk to the car, Louise?" Miss Parker asked.

"Of course!"

Louise started off alone but was so unsteady on her feet that Jean rushed to support her. Miss Parker took her other arm. The trio had nearly reached the roadway when they heard an automobile drive away.

"Gracious! I hope that wasn't our car!" exclaimed Miss Parker fearfully.

A few minutes later the three came within view of the road. To their relief, the car was still there.

"Thank goodness!" said the teacher, drawing a deep sigh. "When once we are safely away from this place, I'll think twice before coming back."

"I wonder who just drove away?" Jean speculated.

"It might have been the policeman who ordered Nura out of the inn," Louise suggested.

"Or the person who threw that object at you, Louise," added Miss Parker. "How does your head feel now?"

"Oh, much better, thank you."

The three climbed into the car and Miss Parker took the wheel, after getting the key from Louise.

"I wonder what Mrs. Crandall will say when she learns of your accident, Louise?" the teacher remarked as she started the motor. "She'll probably refuse to allow any of the students to visit the inn."

"Oh, I hope not!" Louise cried out. "Wouldn't it be better if we didn't mention my injury at all, Miss Parker? I'm perfectly all right now—it was just a scratch."

"And the girls at Starhurst would love to see the old inn, I know," Jean said persuasively. "It would be a shame to put a genuine historical landmark like that 'off limits.' Think how much we could all learn about Civil War architecture from it!"

"And wouldn't it be fascintaing to learn more about the history and legends of the old place," Louise urged.

Miss Parker's courage seemed to return suddenly. "I think you girls are right," she said. "From the glimpse I had, I'm sure the inside of the building must be interesting. I'd like to bring my American history classes here. But I won't consider it until I'm certain the place is absolutely safe."

"We'll make it safe!" Jean promised rashly.

The car was moving slowly around a curve. Louise half turned in her seat to glance toward the woods. Back among the trees, she saw a flash of bright color.

"It's Nura!" Louise cried excitedly. "She wants us to stop!"

The gypsy girl stood on a rise of land, waving a kerchief to attract their attention.

"Maybe it's a trick," suggested Miss Parker uneasily. "We'd better go on."

"Oh, I don't think that it's a trick," Jean insisted. "Maybe Nura knows who struck Louise. She may have something important to tell us."

"Please, let's stop," urged Louise. "We can be on our guard."

Reluctantly their chaperone brought the car to a standstill at the edge of the road. To their amazement, Nura did not move down the slope to join the group. Instead, she kept beckoning to them from the woods.

"Come! Please!" she called in a soft, pleading voice. "I need your help. Follow me!"

CHAPTER VI

Trickery?

As LOUISE and Jean started to climb from the car, Miss Parker caught their arms.

"No, girls. Don't go. I'm sure that it's a trick."

"But Nura acts as if she's sincere," Louise pleaded. "If she did tell us the truth, she probably needs our help. I hate to leave without talking to her."

"Then let her come to us," the teacher said. "We'll wait and see what happens."

Nura kept beckoning and calling for nearly a minute. When she realized that Miss Parker and the two girls were not going to heed the summons to follow her, she seemed undecided about what to do. Finally she came slowly down the slope to the car.

From a pocket between the folds of her full skirt Nura took out an old silver bracelet. She flashed the exquisite piece of jewelry before the astonished eyes of her onlookers.

"Please help me," she said simply. "In return, I will give you this."

Louise and Jean were a bit shocked by the gypsy's offer. They assured her that they never expected any rewards for giving help to people who needed it.

"A *gajo* would help a gypsy without pay?" Nura asked in amazement.

"Of course," Louise assured her. "That doesn't enter into it."

"Then you will help me?"

"That depends," Louise returned cautiously. "Suppose you tell me first what happened in the woods when I was knocked out."

A shocked expression came over the gypsy girl's face as she noticed the swelling. "You were knocked out? How?"

Louise explained, and Nura said she was sorry but had no idea who had caused the injury.

"Maybe you think it was a gypsy?" she asked, worried. "I am sure it was not."

"If we should help you, what would you want us to do, Nura?"

"Help me find the stolen skafidi. If I can return that to the tribe, it will clear Stivo's name and my father will let me marry him."

"Finding the skafidi sounds like a pretty big order," remarked Jean. "We don't even know what the tray looks like."

"I can draw you a picture of it," Nura offered.

"That would help," Jean conceded. "Have you any idea what might have become of the silver tray?"

"The skafidi has great value. It has been sold by now, I think, or pawned."

"We might check the pawnbrokers' shops for you," Louise remarked thoughtfully. Then she added, "Did you drop a spoon in the woods?"

"A spoon? No. Why?"

Louise did not say that she thought it might have been dropped by the person who had injured her and might be a clue to his identity. Instead, she merely told of Jean's find, and after describing the spoon, asked:

"Did anyone in your tribe own such a spoon?"

Nura shook her head. Then Jean told about the legend of the curse. The gypsy girl said that she had never heard the story, although Romany lore was full of such tales.

"Nura," said Louise, "is your tribe camping near here?"

"About ten miles away, near Franklyn," the girl answered. "You would like to visit my people?"

"If we're to help you find the skafidi, I think we should talk to other members of your tribe."

Nura's lips parted in a flashing smile. "Then you mean to help me?"

"We don't want to promise yet, but we'll try,"

Louise replied cautiously after a warning look from Miss Parker. "If you've left your people, I suppose it would be difficult for you to arrange a meeting for us with your father."

"No," the gypsy girl said quickly. "It will be easy. Sebenca will arrange it."

"Sebenca?" Jean repeated.

"Our finest fortuneteller. She is a good friend of mine and Stivo's, too." Nura laughed. "Gajos take her for a witch and sometimes are afraid to let her tell their fortunes. That is because she is so old and wrinkled. But she is really a very kind and generous person."

Uncertain as to whether or not they could get permission from Mrs. Crandall to visit a gypsy camp, Louise and Jean consulted Miss Parker.

"I'm sure that the headmistress never would allow you to go there alone," the teacher said.

"But with you?" Jean suggested.

"Well, it might be arranged if I spoke to Mrs. Crandall."

"That's wonderful," the Danas said together, then Louise added, "Nura, suppose you arrange for us to visit the gypsy camp. When can we see you again?"

"Tomorrow. At this same hour."

"We'll try to make it," Louise promised. "Tell Sebenca we'll be there the day after tomorrow."

She noticed, then, that the gypsy girl's attention

had been suddenly diverted. She stood rigid as a statue, staring at the dense woods on the opposite side of the road.

Following her gaze, the others were startled to see the upper half of a face framed momentarily in the screen of light-green leaves. Someone was watching! As they tried to distinguish the features, the face vanished.

"Was that someone you know, Nura?" Louise asked.

But Nura did not reply. Without even saying good-by, she turned and ran off.

"Well, how odd!" Miss Parker exclaimed. "Why did she run away?"

"Nura was frightened, I think," Louise said. "I wonder who that was looking at us."

"Let's investigate," Jean urged.

"Oh, please don't start off through the woods again," Miss Parker pleaded nervously. "Remember what happened last time, Louise."

"I'm not likely to forget," Louise said, gingerly touching the sore spot on her forehead. "I promise we'll only walk along the edge of the woods."

Thus reassured, the teacher permitted the sisters to search. She remained at the wheel, anxiously watching as they scrambled up a slight incline. Jean led the way directly to the place where they had glimpsed the prying eyes.

No one was there. In the soft earth, however, the girls found several footprints.

"These were made by a woman's shoe," she asserted.

"Yes, with flat heels—almost like ours," Louise added, peering at the imprints. "Let's see where they go."

"Okay. Do you think that someone may have followed Nura?"

"Or us," was Louise's startling reply.

The sisters traced the footprints for a short distance. Then Louise stopped.

"We mustn't go any deeper into the woods," she warned. "Miss Parker will be worried."

"I hate to give up," said Jean, "but I suppose a promise is a promise."

Louise chuckled. "We're in luck, Jean. These footprints run parallel to the road from here."

The girls followed them eagerly, with Miss Parker trailing in the car. Presently the Danas reached a cleared area. At this point the road curved sharply. Beyond, there were few trees or bushes. Suddenly they caught a glimpse of two young women in the distance. One wore a light-blue skirt, the other a yellow one. The figures were a considerable distance ahead and just disappearing into the shelter of the woods beyond the clearing.

"Were they gypsies?" Jean asked.

Louise was inclined to think that gypsies were not likely to wear such slim, straight skirts.

"You know, the one in the blue skirt looked a little like Lettie Briggs," she said.

Jean gasped. "Lettie was wearing a light-blue skirt today! I noticed it at breakfast, because it's new and good-looking."

"The girl in yellow might have been Ina," Louise speculated. "How was she dressed today?"

"It seems to me she was wearing a yellow skirt," Jean replied. "Shall we follow them?"

The question was answered for the girls by Miss Parker. A honk of the horn informed them that the teacher was impatient to start for Starhurst School. Reluctantly the sisters abandoned the pursuit.

"We'll find out," Jean declared. "Maybe Lettie and Ina were the ones who blew the car horn and did the screaming."

"But I don't think that they'd go so far as to knock me out," Louise remarked.

Back at the dormitory, Louise and Jean hurried to their rooms and started to dress for dinner.

"I certainly picked up a lot of mud on my loafers," Louise remarked, scraping the soles. "They're a mess."

"Mine, too," Jean said, putting on fresh stockings and a pair of pumps. "Say, Louise, you've given me an idea!"

"About what?"

"Lettie and Ina. If they were at the crossroads this afternoon, why wouldn't their shoes have mud on them, too?"

"They certainly would!" Louise chuckled. "It hasn't rained lately, but those paths deep in the woods were as soggy as if it had."

Jean glanced at an ivory clock on the dressing table. "If I hurry I'll just have time to peek into the girls' wardrobe closet before dinner."

"Lettie and Ina may not leave their room until just before the dinner gong," Louise remarked.

"I'll see in a few minutes." Having made up her mind to inspect Lettie's closet, Jean finished dressing quickly. She was just about to leave the room when Louise stopped her.

"Jean, what did you do with that spoon you found at the crossroads? I thought you left it on the dressing table."

"I did."

"It's not here now," Louise said.

"Maybe Mattie put the spoon away when she cleaned the room," Jean suggested.

"I've already searched."

Looking back from the doorway, Jean was startled to see a worried expression on her sister's face.

"The spoon is gone," Louise said quietly. "Jean, I'm afraid someone has taken it!"

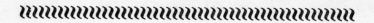

CHAPTER VII

A Summons for Jean

To MAKE sure that the spoon really was missing, Jean
started a search of her own in places Louise had not
examined. The silver piece could not be found anywhere.

"Mattie or any of the other maids—they wouldn't
have taken it," Louise said, deeply worried. "All Mrs.
Crandall's servants are honest."

Jean hesitated to mention a suspicion in her mind,
but finally she said:

"Louise, do you think Lettie or Ina might have
been in here to play a joke on me?"

"It wouldn't be the first time that they've tried it.
And Lettie was miffed because you made those
mumbo-jumbo signs over her."

"Losing the spoon is bad enough," said Jean, "but
there's another problem."

"The danger to the thief?"

48

"Yes. We've made light of the poison risk. Suppose, though, that the person who took the spoon should use it to eat with and something should happen?"

"It might be fatal if the legend is true!" Louise exclaimed.

"We must tell Mrs. Crandall at once—that is, if Lettie and Ina don't confess."

"I'll bet they will. Look!" Jean exclaimed. "Someone with muddy shoes was in here." She pointed out the faint but visible marks. "Our shoes didn't make those prints."

"No. We took ours off when we came into the study," Louise said.

"It looks bad for Lettie and Ina," her sister declared.

"Well, if they have the spoon, at least they know about the poison," Louise reminded her.

"Lettie thought we were joking about that," Jean declared. "She's so headstrong, she may just ignore our warning."

Jean went at once to the girls' room. They were not in it, nor were they on the first floor. Jean questioned several girls who were there, but none of them had seen Lettie or Ina, and they knew nothing about the spoon.

"I *must* go to Mrs. Crandall," Jean decided. "I haven't much time, either. The dinner bell will ring any minute."

She hurried to the headmistress's apartment and

quickly told her of the theft. Mrs. Crandall became upset.

"Poison!" she cried. "Oh, dear, this is most distressing. Now I must announce the loss of the spoon at dinner. It will be especially embarrassing since Professor Stanley is to be our guest."

"John Stanley, the lecturer?" Jean asked, recalling Miss Parker's mention of the traveler.

"Yes, he is going to speak after dinner in the lounge. His subject will be European Influence on Early New England Witchcraft. We are most fortunate to have such a distinguished lecturer at Starhurst. What will he think when I announce that a silver spoon has been taken?"

"Perhaps we could wait—" Jean began dubiously.

Mrs. Crandall brushed aside any suggestion of delay. "No, you were right in coming to me at once," she said. "The matter is most serious. We must recover the spoon."

At that moment the dinner gong sounded. Jean joined Louise and told her about her talk with Mrs. Crandall. They walked into the large dining room with the other students. Already it was buzzing with whispered comments, for Professor Stanley's presence at the head table had been noted immediately.

"Handsome, isn't he?" the Danas heard Lettie say with a giggle as they passed her and took their places at the next table.

Louise and Jean were not as impressed by the new-comer's appearance as Lettie was. He was an ordinary-looking man of about forty, with sharp features, unruly black hair, and eyes that seemed to bore through one.

A few minutes later, while the professor was waiting for Mrs. Crandall to introduce him, he kept plucking nervously at a tiny mustache.

"I wonder where he's from?" speculated Evelyn Starr, who was sitting next to Louise.

"I heard he came here through a lecture bureau," replied Doris Harland across the table.

Mrs. Crandall rose as a signal for quiet. First, she introduced Professor Stanley, praising his accomplishments in glowing terms.

Louise noted that in speaking of the lecturer's background the headmistress offered few specific facts, although the list of his various degrees was quite impressive.

After urging all the students to attend the reception to be given for their guest before the required lecture, Mrs. Crandall brought up the matter of the missing spoon. Without stressing the loss more than was necessary, she briefly described the antique silver piece and told of its poison properties.

"The spoon must be returned to Jean Dana or my office without delay," she concluded. "Otherwise, it will be necessary for me to question students individually. I sincerely trust that such drastic action will not be necessary."

While the headmistress was speaking, Jean turned slightly and kept close watch of Lettie. The girl sat with a fixed smile on her lips. Winking at Ina, she whispered rather loudly:

"That's all nonsense about the spoon being poisoned! Jean and Louise made up that story just to be the center of attention."

"But if it should be true—" Ina began.

"Hush!" Lettie warned, suddenly noticing that Jean was watching her. "You talk too much, Ina!"

More than ever, Louise and Jean were suspicious that Lettie knew what had become of the missing piece of silver. They were equally certain that she would not return it unless forced to do so.

After dinner they tried to talk to her about the spoon. Lettie scornfully refused to discuss the matter.

"In another minute you'll be accusing *me* of taking your trashy old silver," she said. With a toss of her head, she started to walk off.

"Lettie, we're trying to warn you for your own good," Louise replied earnestly. "That story about the spoon being impregnated with poison is true."

"Tell me another good one!" With a shrug, Lettie moved off to join a group of students who were clustered around Professor Stanley.

"Why don't we search her room?" proposed Evelyn Starr, who had overheard the conversation with Lettie.

"I'd planned to do that very thing—for two reasons," Jean confided.

"If you went now, Lettie would be sure to notice your absence and probably trail you," Louise remarked.

"I'll tell you what. Suppose you and Doris stay here in the lounge and watch Lettie and Ina," Jean suggested. "Evelyn and I can do the sleuthing."

"All right," Louise agreed. "You'd better work fast, though. Professor Stanley is due to start his lecture in twenty minutes."

Jean and Evelyn managed to slip away without attracting any attention, and went directly to the rooms shared by Lettie and Ina. As usual, the place was very untidy. Jean smiled as she saw a light-blue skirt and a yellow one on the beds. There were muddy spots on the rug near the door. Jean told Evelyn her suspicions.

"I'd say they were out at the crossroads all right," Evelyn said.

While she searched for the missing antique spoon, Jean examined the closet. Shoes had been tossed helter-skelter.

Even so, her search was well worth while. She found two pairs of shoes which were coated with fresh-caked mud.

"This proves it!" Jean said to herself. "The next

thing is to find out just what those two were doing at the crossroads."

By this time, Evelyn had completed her search of everything but the desk drawers. "If the spoon is here, it's too well hidden to be found quickly," she reported.

"We'd better go," Jean decided, quickly replacing the shoes in the closet. "The lecture will start soon. Anyway, I've learned one thing!"

"What, Jean?"

"That Lettie and Ina were prowling around the old inn today."

"And without permission, I'll bet," said Evelyn. "Whatever made them go there?"

"Oh, you know Lettie," Jean answered. "It's just her natural curiosity. I'm afraid that even though we were so careful she may still have overheard us talking about where I found the silver spoon and went there hoping to find one herself."

Making certain that the hallway was clear, the two friends left the room and started downstairs to rejoin Louise and Evelyn. On the first landing, they met Martha Frost, a day student in the sophomore class. Her parents were away, so she was staying at Starhurst for a couple of weeks. She was a shy, pretty girl whom the Danas did not know well.

"Oh, Jean," she said, "I have a message for you from your sister."

"A message?"

"You are to meet her in the pantry alone. Go down by the back stairs."

"That's an odd request," Evelyn said, glancing questioningly at Jean. "Why the pantry?"

"I can't imagine," Jean answered. "But I'll go. Thank you, Martha."

"I'll run along down to the lounge," Evelyn said. "See you later."

Puzzled by Louise's request, Jean climbed the steps and walked down the second-floor hallway to the rear staircase which led to the service quarters.

The staircase, an enclosed one, was narrow and dark. Jean groped for a light switch but could not find one. She descended cautiously, feeling for the steps with her toe.

Reaching the first floor, she felt her way across a narrow hallway and found the handle to the pantry door. Suddenly Jean heard a sound behind her and turned quickly. She could see nothing. The next instant, a blanket was thrown over her head and she stumbled to the floor.

Wildly the imprisoned girl struggled to free herself, but the blanket was wrapped so tightly about her that her efforts were futile. She screamed but the sounds were too muffled to be heard.

Suddenly Jean felt herself being moved. Someone was dragging her away!

CHAPTER VIII

A Dream Explained

AFTER leaving Jean, Evelyn Starr had gone down to the lounge with Martha. The lecture had not yet started, and students were still clustered around Professor Stanley.

Entering the crowded room, Evelyn was amazed to see Louise talking to Doris Harland. She hurried over to them.

"Louise, Jean is waiting for you," she whispered.

"Waiting for me? Where?"

"Why, in the pantry as you asked her to," Evelyn answered.

"The pantry? I didn't ask her to meet me there, Evelyn."

The other girl gulped in dismay. "You mean you didn't send word by Martha Frost asking Jean to join you there alone?"

"No. I haven't even talked to Martha."

56

Evelyn looked frightened. "But Martha brought the message only a moment ago!"

"Something's wrong," Louise declared, frowning. "It may be only a joke, but it could be something more serious. Where's Martha?"

"She was here a minute ago," Evelyn replied, glancing about the lounge room. But she did not see the girl.

"Never mind, we'll talk to her later," Louise said. "Right now, it's more important to find Jean. Oh, I hope it's nothing more than a joke!"

"Perpetrated by Lettie and Ina?" Evelyn suggested.

"Possibly. But they haven't left this room. Doris and I kept them in sight every minute you were gone. Lettie's been trying to monopolize Professor Stanley!"

Louise and Evelyn hurried to the pantry. Jean was not there, and none of the servants had seen her.

Evelyn had flicked on the light switch outside the pantry's rear door. There was no sign of Jean on the back stairs. A door which led to the outside gave Louise an idea.

"Jean may have gone into the yard," she commented. "I wish we had a flashlight. It's too dark out there to see much."

As Louise peered into the dimly lighted service yard at the rear of the dormitory she thought she heard a muffled cry.

"What was that?" she cried.

"I couldn't tell," Evelyn replied, listening intently. "The sound was certainly smothered."

"Jean!" Louise called. "Jean! Are you here?"

"Help! Help!" came the faint cry.

This time the two girls decided that the call had come from beyond the yard and ran toward the gate. Just as they opened it, Jean stumbled toward them. She had freed herself from the blanket shroud, and carried it draped on her shoulders. Her hair was tousled and her clothes wrinkled.

"Jean! What happened? Why are you out here with a blanket?"

"I—I was nearly kidnaped in this blanket," Jean answered shakily. "It nearly smothered me, but I fought so hard that whoever was dragging me let me go."

"How dreadful! Who did it?" Evelyn asked indignantly, while Louise, greatly concerned, put a comforting arm around her sister.

"I don't know," Jean admitted. "It happened so fast I didn't see who it was—besides, it was dark in the hallway. Louise, if you'd only come sooner. Why did you want to meet me in the pantry?"

Louise explained the hoax, then said, "I want to examine that blanket."

Taking it into the hallway under the ceiling light, she looked at it carefully.

"It doesn't belong to the school," she stated.

All Starhurst blankets had the school name woven into the cloth. This one had no identifying marks, but it was very attractive. It was hand-loomed in bright colors to form a hunting scene.

"You know, this looks to me like a gypsy blanket," Louise said.

"If it was a gypsy who tried to harm Jean," said Evelyn, "we should notify the police."

"First, let's talk to Martha. She may be able to throw some light on the mystery."

The girls hurried up the back stairs and carried the blanket to the Dana suite. Jean hurriedly combed her hair, then accompanied Louise and Evelyn to the lounge. Although still inwardly shaken from her experience, Jean gave no indication of it as she mingled with the other students.

After a brief search, the three girls found Martha Frost. Drawing her aside, they told her about the hoax and asked why she had delivered the fake message to Jean.

"You certainly didn't receive any such directions from me," Louise said.

"Why, no," Martha readily admitted. "The message came to me indirectly."

"From whom?"

"I don't exactly recall. Alice Heady, I think, handed me the note. But it was given to her by another student who didn't want to take the time to find Jean."

"Where is the note?" Louise asked.

"I threw it in the incinerator. The wording seemed unimportant. As I remember, it just said 'Meet me in the pantry. Come alone, by the back stairs.' It was signed with your name, Louise."

"Too bad you destroyed the note," Jean commented regretfully. "The handwriting might have been a clue."

"I never dreamed that it was all a trick," Martha said a bit nervously. "I hope you don't think I was mixed up in it."

"Not at all," Jean assured her. "But if you don't mind, please don't say a word about this to anyone, Martha."

"Oh, I won't," the girl promised.

Just then Mrs. Crandall announced that it was time for the lecture to start. With the other students, Jean and Louise walked to the auditorium.

Professor Stanley addressed the group for forty-five minutes, reading every word of his lengthy speech from several sheets of paper. Jean, who had trouble keeping awake, noticed that even Mrs. Crandall seemed rather bored by the dull lecture.

Nevertheless, when the talk ended, many students gathered around the professor to ask questions. As Louise and Jean politely joined the others, they heard Lettie Briggs say excitedly to Ina:

"Professor Stanley has just told me he's an expert

at revealing the meaning of dreams! Isn't that re-markable?"

"Why don't you have him interpret that nightmare you had last night?" Ina asked unpleasantly. "You know, about how you flunked three subjects."

"Maybe that wasn't a dream," suggested Doris imp-ishly, and Lettie threw her a withering look.

The information that Professor Stanley claimed an ability to explain dreams was most interesting to Jean. Quickly a plan came to mind. She whispered to Louise, Evelyn, and Doris that she intended to try an experiment.

"I want you girls to study the faces of all our class-mates," she directed. "Watch their reactions as I tell the professor about *my* recent nightmare."

The girls were puzzled, but agreed. Jean, awaiting her turn to talk with Professor Stanley, soberly in-quired if it were true he could tell the hidden meaning of dreams.

"Ah, yes," he answered, twisting the ends of his little mustache.

"Would you be willing to interpret a dream for me?" she asked engagingly.

Professor Stanley gazed intently into Jean's eyes. He frowned.

"It is rather late now. Some other time perhaps—"

"Now!" pleaded the other students. "Please inter-pret Jean's dream for her!"

Professor Stanley shrugged. "Very well," he agreed reluctantly. "But please be brief."

Jean recounted her adventure on the dark staircase, relating the true facts as if she had dreamed them the previous night. During the recital, Louise, Doris, and Evelyn watched the faces of the other students intently. They noticed that Lettie and Ina seemed ill at ease. But for that matter, several other girls appeared uncomfortable, too, as Jean vividly described her experience.

Professor Stanley listened attentively, his sharp-featured face a cold, hard mask. "Young lady," he demanded when she finished, "didn't you make up that story?"

"I did not make up one word of it," Jean stated firmly. "How do you interpret the dream, Professor?"

The lecturer hesitated. Then, speaking fast, he said in an offhand way:

"The dream has no great significance, except that it expresses a hidden, subconscious fear. You, young lady, are evidently afraid that you will be harmed because you are keeping a secret for someone else."

"A secret?" Jean questioned quickly. "What kind of secret? For whom?"

The lecturer pretended not hear the questions. Staring hard at her, he went on in carefully measured words:

"For your own peace of mind and safety, I advise

you to dismiss this dream of yours from your mind. *Forget the entire affair.* You understand?"

Jean was given no opportunity to reply. At that moment Professor Crandall joined the visitor.

"Come, come, girls," he said, starting to escort the lecturer from the platform, "you must not plague Professor Stanley with your questions about dreams."

"But he was telling us such fascinating things!" declared Alice Heady, her eyes sparkling. "All about a secret that Jean is keeping!"

"Tell us your secret, Jean!" the students begged her, and one girl asked teasingly, "Is it really true that you have one?"

"In a way, yes," Jean admitted, smiling.

"Tell us!" the girls chorused.

Jean laughed but refused to say any more. She had no intention of mentioning the Crossroads Inn or her meeting with the gypsy girl Nura.

"I guess Jean's secret can't be much," Ina Mason scoffed.

"And it's no secret, either," boldly announced Lettie Briggs. Annoyed because Jean had drawn so much attention to herself, Lettie was determined to seize a share of the spotlight.

"What do you mean, Lettie?" Doris called out. "Do you know Jean's secret?"

"I certainly do," Lettie boasted. "Furthermore, if she won't tell you what it is, I will!"

CHAPTER IX

A Denial

AFRAID that Lettie would blurt out some false information about the crossroads mystery, Louise cried out, "Lettie, please—"

Before she could finish the sentence, Professor Stanley, to her amazement, spoke up sharply, "Enough of this talk about dreams!" Looking squarely at Lettie, he added, "You heard Professor Crandall tell you to stop it."

"But you brought up the subject yourself," Lettie countered. "I was only going to tell—"

"Secrets are not to be discussed," the lecturer said severely.

Turning his back upon the students, he moved away with Professor Crandall. Lettie looked very uncomfortable and went toward a little-used exit of the auditorium. The Danas hurried toward her.

"Now that we're by ourselves," said Jean, "what was it you were going to tell, Lettie? What's this big secret you think I'm keeping for someone?"

"Wouldn't you like to know?" Lettie answered flippantly.

"I certainly would."

"Well, go ask a mind reader then! Or a gypsy fortuneteller!"

"What do you mean by that remark?" Jean flared.

"That's for you to find out—if you can," Lettie replied smugly. "I'm not revealing anything."

"You were willing to tell your mysterious information to all the girls a few minutes ago," Jean reminded her. "Why the quick change?"

"I have my reasons."

"Afraid of Professor Stanley?" Jean suggested.

"Certainly not!" Lettie's eyes flashed. "What he said had no effect upon me whatsoever."

Jean smiled. "Then maybe you're afraid Louise and I will tell Mrs. Crandall that you know something about the stolen silver spoon!"

Lettie paled. "You—you wouldn't dare!"

"Or maybe you'd rather have us tell her we saw you in the woods near the Crossroads Inn," Louise put in. "Without permission too, I'll bet."

"You're only saying that," Lettie muttered, backing away. "You're fishing for information. Actually, you don't know a thing."

"Don't we?" Jean laughed. "What about those mud tracks you left in our rooms?"

Hearing this, Lettie looked frightened. She dropped

her blustering manner and said, "You girls aren't tat-tletales. It wouldn't be good sportsmanship to get me into trouble with Mrs. Crandall."

Jean had not intended to tell the headmistress her suspicions, but she led Lettie on, hoping to find out what she might have learned about the gypsy girl.

"We won't report you if you make a full confession," Jean promised.

"I've nothing to confess."

"Weren't you at the crossroads today? You and Ina?"

"Maybe we did take a little ride in that general direction," Lettie admitted reluctantly. "Any harm in a taxi ride?"

"Not if you had permission."

"What if we didn't? It was an important trip. I wanted to learn—"

"Yes?" Louise prompted as Lettie broke off, aware that she was saying too much.

"I'm in the midst of solving a mystery," Lettie announced grandly. "But don't ask me any questions about it, because I won't tell you!"

Unnoticed by Louise and Jean, Ina Mason had come up quietly behind the trio. Hearing her roommate's last remarks, she laughed.

"That's a howl! *You* solving a mystery, Lettie Briggs! I thought—"

"Be quiet!" Lettie ordered. "You *don't* think, Ina, that's just the trouble. I'll do the talking."

"You always do," Ina complained. "I never get in a word."

"We were just asking Lettie about your being in our rooms today after you two got back from the woods," Louise remarked.

Ina winced. "It was all Lettie's idea," she said. "I didn't want to do either of them."

"Will you hush?" her roommate broke in angrily. With a quick change of tone, Lettie admitted to Louise and Jean that they had been in the suite a minute or so. "I wanted to use your Spanish dictionary, Louise," she explained.

"The library has a much better one," Jean spoke up.

"I didn't think of that," Lettie said glibly.

"You're sure that you didn't take the silver spoon?" Jean asked, looking searchingly into the other's eyes.

"You're accusing me of stealing?"

"I didn't say that, Lettie. We thought you might have been playing a joke on us. You understand, don't you, that the loss of the spoon is a serious matter? Someone may become ill as a consequence."

"Yes, I know. But I didn't take it, and that's the truth. You can search my room if you don't believe me."

The Danas suppressed a smile and did not reveal that Jean already had been there. "That won't be necessary," Louise replied.

"You can ask Ina if we know anything about your old spoon," Lettie went on pettishly.

"Suppose you tell us why you were in our room," Jean suggested. "You can't expect us to believe that story about the Spanish dictionary."

"The truth is, Ina and I slipped in hoping to play a little joke on you," Lettie confessed. "We didn't have time to pull it off. You got back from the crossroads too soon. That's all there is to the story."

"Every single bit," echoed Ina.

Although Lettie often distorted the truth, the sisters did believe her now.

"We'll accept your word," Louise said. "But please, Lettie, if you learn what became of the spoon, do tell us or Mrs. Crandall."

"All right."

Later that night, as Louise and Jean prepared for bed, they speculated upon the nature of the joke Lettie had intended to play, and what she might know about Nura and the gypsy mystery.

"I hope Lettie hasn't heard about the stolen skafidi," Jean remarked, jumping into bed. "If she starts trying to find that, she may make it difficult for us to solve the mystery."

"Lettie already knows too much, I'm afraid." Louise sighed. "Now that her curiosity is aroused, she won't stop until she learns everything possible."

"But that doesn't bother me as much as the loss of the spoon," Jean confessed.

Hopeful that Mrs. Crandall might have some news about it, the sisters went to her office directly after breakfast the next morning. The headmistress reported that the silver piece had not been found at the school. Every student and every servant had denied seeing it.

"Let's hope that the spoon no longer bears a trace of poison," she commented anxiously. "The whole affair disturbs me very much."

Louise was about to ask if Miss Parker had yet requested permission for the sisters to go to the gypsy camp, when the telephone rang. Since it was a long-distance call, the girls discreetly left.

"I'd like to begin working on the mystery right away," Jean said to her sister as they climbed the stairs to their rooms.

"Let's check jewelry stores, gift shops, secondhand stores, and pawnshops for miles around," Louise suggested. "We can telephone some of them between classes."

"All right. I'll start as soon as English history class is over."

Throughout the morning the sisters took turns calling. Jean began by checking telephone books and writing down the name and phone number of every firm that looked halfway promising. The list was an imposing one.

"This is a bigger task than I thought it would be," she told Louise at lunchtime.

"No use doing it, though, unless we're thorough and cover every possible place."

Since Miss Parker could not accompany them to

see Nura, and Mrs. Crandall had refused permission for them to go alone, the girls continued their telephoning after classes.

Working systematically, the girls finally contacted every shop on the list. At each establishment they were assured that no silver tray or unusual old jewelry had been brought in recently.

"Well, that's that," Jean remarked at the end of the afternoon but refused to be discouraged by their failure. "Tracing that silver tray will be a real job."

"Yes," Louise agreed. "The person who took that tray may have sold it in another state."

"That's possible." Jean nodded. "Particularly if the thief's a wandering gypsy. Or, for that matter, it might still be in his possession."

That evening Doris and Evelyn came into the Danas' suite just before study hours, bearing a big basket of fruit.

"Oh, wonderful!" Jean exclaimed. "Where did you get it?"

"Dad brought it to me this afternoon," Doris replied. "It's a kind of peace offering."

"Peace offering?" Louise echoed, smiling.

"*Mmm*," Doris mumbled, biting into a huge apple. "Dad had forgotten to send me any allowance for the last two weeks! I was desperate!"

"Well, let's hope he forgets it regularly from now on," Jean remarked as she peeled a tangerine. Doris threw a pillow at her.

Later that evening as Louise was brushing her hair she brought up the subject of the mystery again. "I wonder what Nura thinks of our not showing up at the crossroads today?"

"No use worrying about it tonight," Jean replied with a yawn. "Put up the window and let's get some sleep. The 'lights-out' bell will ring in five minutes."

Louise opened the window and leaned out. Resting her arms on the sill, she breathed deeply several times.

"You know, Jean," she said, "you were right. It does smell *green* out!"

"Fine," Jean replied. "Now switch off that light and come to bed!"

Reluctantly Louise obeyed and Jean snapped off the bed lamp. As Louise was adjusting the venetian blind, she suddenly jerked back. A small, hard object sailed past her head and fell to the floor.

"What was that?" Jean cried, switching on the bedside light again.

Louise quickly picked up the object.

"Why, it's a flat stone!" she exclaimed. "And there's a paper fastened to it with a rubber band!"

Jean watched excitedly as Louise slipped off the band and unfolded the paper.

"Jean," Louise cried, "it's a note for us from Nura!"

CHAPTER X

Danger

EAGERLY the Dana girls pored over the brief message that had been tossed through the open window of their bedroom. It was written in a bold, almost illegible scrawl and said:

I must see you at once secretly. Nura.

After switching off the bed light, Louise hurried back to the window and looked out. She could see no one below.

"Do you suppose this note is another hoax?" she asked Jean, who had joined her.

Her sister shrugged. "If it wasn't Nura, it could have been a messenger."

"Whoever it was is keeping out of sight," Louise said. "Well, let's watch."

For several minutes the two girls sat by the window in the darkened room, but no one appeared on the grounds.

"This is certainly strange," Jean commented.

72

"What did Nura mean? That we go outside? Come on, let's go!"

"But how can we?" Louise asked. "It's against the rules to leave the building after the 'lights-out' signal, and the bell will ring any second now."

"I'd like to take a chance just the same," her sister said.

"We're not even certain Nura wrote the note, Jean."

"Yes, it could be a trick of Lettie's to get even with us. She was peeved that we found out about her trip to the crossroads."

"Lettie would love to have Mrs. Crandall catch us breaking a rule." Louise nodded. "I hate to ignore this note, though. It might be genuine."

"I know!" Jean cried, jumping up in sudden inspiration. "The rose trellis at the end of the hall!"

"What about it?"

"It's easy to climb."

"A number of students have done it." Louise grinned. "Some were caught, too. No, thanks, Jean. We mustn't take the risk of going down that way."

"Oh, I don't mean for us to do it! This is my idea, Louise. Why not toss out a message saying we'll meet the writer of that note at the top of the trellis as soon as lights are out?"

"If the person who threw the note isn't around, the watchman will find it later. But I guess it would be safe enough if we don't sign it."

Hastily the two girls turned on a light, composed a note, and fastened it to the flat stone. Louise snapped off the light as Jean tossed the message to the lawn below. Then they stood waiting. The retiring bell rang.

"No one seems to be around," Louise declared when several minutes had elapsed and the note remained where it had fallen in the lush spring grass.

"I guess we may as well go to bed," Jean decided.

One by one lamps went out in the dormitory until only those in the halls were left to cast their yellow pools on the lawn.

Jean stood up, stretched, and turned from the window. Just then Louise touched her arm.

"Those bushes over there—" she whispered. "They're moving!"

Jean turned back to the window just in time to see a long stick slide out of the shrubbery. It inched slowly toward the note, then quickly raked it back to the shelter of the bushes.

"Someone has it!" Jean said jubilantly. "Now let's go down the hall to the balcony and wait."

"We must be quiet," Louise warned. "We're supposed to be in bed."

The dimly lighted corridor was deserted, but from the floor above, the sisters could hear monitors checking the rooms to make sure that all the students had retired. Louise and Jean estimated that they might have a margin of fifteen to twenty minutes before their rooms were checked. Putting on robes and slippers, the girls hurried down the hall, unlocked the balcony window, and stepped out. They peered anxiously below.

"See anyone?" Jean whispered.

"Not yet."

Several minutes passed. The night air was becoming chilly and the girls began to shiver.

"I don't believe anyone is coming," Louise finally said. "We'd better return to our rooms before we're checked as absent."

"Wait!" Jean whispered, as she glimpsed a shadow moving around the corner of the building. "Someone is coming now!"

"A gypsy girl!" Jean said tensely, noting the full, swaying skirt and long, dark hair. "It really is Nura!"

The gypsy girl did not hesitate. Seizing the wooden support, she began to climb swiftly. She was halfway up when the school watchman ambled around the corner of the building. The beam of his flashlight focused plainly upon the climbing girl.

"Hey, you!" he shouted. "Come down off that trellis!"

Nura, terrified, paused. To the consternation of the Danas, the old watchman started climbing the wooden support. He seized Nura, who squirmed like an eel in his grasp.

"No! No! You're making a mistake!" Louise called down to the watchman. "Wait—let her go!"

"What's that?" the man cried, looking up in amazement.

His grasp loosened on Nura's arm. Quick as a flash, she pulled free and leaped lightly to the ground. The next instant she dashed around the corner of the building out of view.

The old watchman scrambled down the trellis as fast as his age would permit. Muttering angrily, he took off after the fleet-footed girl.

On the balcony above, Louise and Jean were startled to hear soft padding footsteps in the dormitory hall. Before they could crawl back through the window, Lettie Briggs confronted them.

"I thought I heard voices! What's going on here?"

"*Sh!*" Jean warned. "Not so loud!"

Quickly she and Louise crawled back through the window, closing it behind them.

"You've been out of the building!" Lettie accused.

"No, we haven't," Jean corrected. "We were only enjoying a bit of air on the balcony."

"You can't fool me! I saw and heard everything!"

Louise and Jean wondered just how much Lettie had seen of the incident, but they had no chance to find out. Just then, they heard Mrs. Crandall's quick footsteps on the nearby staircase!

The Danas scooted for their suite and reached the study only a moment before the headmistress came into view. Dashing into the bedroom, the girls made a dive for their beds, and pretended to be asleep.

Mrs. Crandall peered in through the half-opened door as she went by. Then she walked to the end of the corridor, where Lettie stood trapped. Since her room was near the stairway, she had had no chance to escape.

"Lettie, what are you doing here?" the headmistress asked her severely. "Why aren't you in your room?"

"All the noise and shouting woke me up. The Dana girls were trying to help someone up the rose trellis," Lettie said. "You must have heard them yelling and screaming."

"Indeed, I didn't. I heard your voice, Lettie. That was why I came up to investigate."

"Well, investigate Louise and Jean," Lettie replied crossly. "They unlocked this window and sneaked out on the balcony to meet someone."

Mrs. Crandall inspected the window. Seeing that it was unlocked, she looked out, then fastened the catch. Turning to Lettie, she said:

"Please return to your room at once!"

"Well, I like that!" Lettie muttered indignantly. "I guess you think I'm not telling you the truth. Just check on Louise and Jean—"

"I already have. They are asleep."

"I tell you they were meeting someone on the balcony! Why don't you ask the watchman if he saw anyone?"

"The watchman will report any such incident to

me. But frankly, Lettie, I think you must have dreamed all this. No one is near the trellis. Now go to your room at once, or I'll be compelled to deny you social privileges for a week."

"Yes, Mrs. Crandall," Lettie mumbled.

Louise and Jean remained motionless in their beds. They half expected that the headmistress would return to make a few inquiries as to their escapade.

"We'll have to tell her about Nura," Louise whispered. "The watchman will report the whole thing, anyway."

"Do you think he saw us?" Jean asked.

"Maybe not, but Lettie will fill in that detail, you can be sure."

"Well, if Mrs. Crandall doesn't come back, let's wait until tomorrow and explain the whole affair," Jean suggested.

The headmistress did not revisit the Danas and presently returned to her own apartment. Still excited, Louise and Jean found it impossible to fall asleep. What had happened to Nura, they wondered. Had she managed to get away?

Jean laughed softly. "She was too quick for the old watchman."

"Too bad we didn't have a chance to talk to Nura," Louise said regretfully. "What she wanted to tell us must be pretty important. I wonder if it was about our visit to her people."

"Maybe."

Fifteen minutes passed. Louise finally dozed off, but Jean could not sleep. Restless, she tossed in her bed. Every sound in the quiet dormitory seemed magnified. Even the steady drip, drip of a shower tap some distance away annoyed her.

Getting up, Jean went to tighten the faucet. As she was about to climb into bed once more, she was startled to see an object come hurtling through the open window. She knew instantly that it must be another stone with a note attached.

Louise, awakened by the thud, sat up in bed. "What was that?" she demanded nervously.

"A message, I think!" Jean informed her. "I'll switch on a light."

Louise bounded out of bed as her sister turned on the bed light. Jean unfastened a paper attached to the stone.

"Yes, it's from Nura!" she cried, holding the torn sheet under the light.

"What does she say, Jean? Did she get away safely?"

"She must have, or she wouldn't have dared slip back to hurl this message."

"Read it!" Louise demanded.

" *'Danger at the crossroads!'* " Jean read slowly and emphatically. " *'Do not come. Nura.'* "

CHAPTER XI

The Kerchief's Message

AFTER reading Nura's note that there was new danger at the crossroads, Louise and Jean wondered what had happened there. They reread the note three times, trying to determine its hidden meaning.

"Does she want us to forget all about the mystery?" Jean asked, disappointment in her voice.

"I doubt that," Louise replied. "I believe she'll get in touch with us later."

"I still think we should go to the gypsy camp at Franklyn, anyway, Louise. Miss Parker arranged for the trip tomorrow."

"We'll go, Jean. That is, if Mrs. Crandall will let us after she hears our little confession tomorrow."

Louise leaned out the window once more.

"Any sign of Nura?" Jean asked.

"Not a sign of anyone. I guess Nura fled as soon

as she tossed the stone. At any rate, she wasn't caught by the watchman," Louise said in relief.

"About the trip tomorrow, let's go as early as possible," Jean proposed.

"Suits me," her sister agreed, crawling back into bed. "We'll have to wait for Mrs. Crandall's verdict, though."

After breakfast the next morning, the Danas went to the headmistress's apartment. They came out half an hour later looking sheepish but relieved after telling her of Nura's visit. They had decided not to mention the warning note, for fear Mrs. Crandall would not let them return to the crossroads.

They met Miss Parker in the hall, told her about their conference with the headmistress, and discussed the trip to the gypsy camp.

"You girls are lucky Mrs. Crandall doesn't object to your missing the afternoon session," the teacher said.

"Yes, aren't we?" Jean replied, adding with a giggle, "I can do without my chem experiments and still find out how to blow up the lab!"

"Why, Jean!" Miss Parker reproved her, but with a smile. Jean blushed a little, glad that their young teacher had a sense of humor.

"We can start immediately after my one-thirty class," Miss Parker told the girls. "I'll meet you at the garage."

"We'll be there," Louise promised.

"I hope that Lettie and Ina don't hear about our trip," Jean remarked. "They might decide to tag along."

"They haven't gained an inkling of our plans from me," Miss Parker assured her.

As the three talked, the Danas were surprised to see Professor Stanley sauntering down the corridor. They had assumed that he had left Starhurst School the night before last.

"Oh, no," Miss Parker said when Louise mentioned this. "He will be here for a week."

"A week?" Jean echoed. "Why so long?"

"He suggested to Mrs. Crandall that he stay and give a series of lectures. She consented. He's occupying the first-floor guest room."

Professor Stanley joined the group. After greeting them with a friendly "good morning," he turned to Jean and eyed her intently. "You slept well the past two nights, I trust?" he asked.

"Perfectly."

"Any dreams?"

"I was too sound asleep," Jean returned, but was a trifle nonplused by his insistent staring. She began to edge away.

"Ah, no dreams?" the man pursued the subject. "That means you must have decided to abandon your worrisome secret."

"If I have a worrisome secret, I'm sure I don't know about it," Jean answered.

Taking Louise by the arm, she strolled away. Out of earshot, Jean whispered, "Professor Stanley certainly is a bore."

"I agree."

"All that talk about dreams annoys me," Jean said. "And he gave me the creeps the way he kept staring at me. You know, sometimes I have a queer sort of feeling—"

"Yes?"

"It's silly, I guess." Jean laughed apologetically. "I just get the feeling that he's trying to frighten me. What do you think he means by his chatter about abandoning a worrisome secret?"

"I wonder."

"You don't suppose Lettie could have told him about Nura?"

"Oh, she's probably told him everything she knows," Louise answered. "Fortunately, I don't think she impresses him very much."

Farther along the corridor, the two girls met Professor Crandall. Deeply submerged in his own thoughts, he walked with his head down and did not notice them.

"Good morning, Professor Crandall," the girls said together, and Louise added, "You look rather unhappy this morning. Is something the matter?"

The professor looked up and gazed at the sisters over the top of his glasses.

"Oh, hello, girls," he said absently. "I didn't recognize you for a moment. Yes, something is the matter."

"Can we help you?" Louise asked quickly.

"Perhaps you can. I've misplaced some valuable historical research notes."

Jean and Louise looked at each other. That explained why the professor was so worried and pensive the day of the tournament. However, the loss of the notes did not surprise the Danas, who were accustomed to similar situations due to the professor's forgetfulness.

"I'm sure that they'll turn up," Jean said cheerfully. "Did you have them in your study?"

"I'm sure I left them on top of my desk in the apartment. I put them there with some books a few days ago. When I needed the notes, they were gone."

"You probably moved them to another place," Louise remarked. "One of the drawers, perhaps?"

"I've looked in every one. But there is more to this. The notes aren't the only thing missing. My wallet disappeared too."

"At the same time?"

"No. I'm sure I had it yesterday."

Although Louise and Jean knew that Professor Crandall often misplaced his wallet, they were sympathetic and said they hoped he would locate it soon.

The professor shook his head in bewilderment. "I can't understand it. I'm sure that the wallet was on my highboy."

Jean asked if the wallet had contained very much money.

"About seventy-five dollars. Perhaps it was only fifty," the professor said. "I—I can't recall the exact amount."

The sisters felt sorry for the professor and offered to help him search for the missing wallet and his notes.

"I'll be most grateful if you will," he said, brightening a bit. Then, with a guilty, confiding smile, he said, "Please don't speak of this to Mrs. Crandall. She'll be so upset."

The Danas promised not to mention the loss to the headmistress. For that matter, they were convinced that her husband had merely misplaced both the wallet and the valuable notes. They followed him into his study and searched in all the likely places, then the most unlikely ones, but failed to find the missing articles.

"We'll keep trying," Louise assured the downcast professor. Do you think that you might have left your notes in the school library?"

"I'm sure I didn't."

"Jean and I will check there to make certain. By the way, when did you last have the wallet?"

"It may have been that day I drove you girls to the

tennis tournament. Or was it the day after? I'm not sure."

"You have so many things to think about, Professor Crandall," Louise said kindly, "it isn't surprising that some things get misplaced. It may come to you suddenly where you put the wallet and the papers."

As the Danas left him, Jean said to her sister, "If only the wallet had disappeared, I could almost believe a pickpocket had taken it. But I'm sure no petty thief would want the notes, and Professor Crandall seems to think they disappeared about the same time."

"It's perplexing, all right," Louise conceded. "Mysteries seem to be coming our way lately. But I'm hoping part of one is going to be solved this afternoon."

Shortly after two o'clock the Danas met Miss Parker at the garage and the trio drove off in the Starhurst station wagon.

"Let's take the route that leads past the Crossroads Inn," Jean proposed. "If Nura sees our car, she may come out and speak to us."

Louise gave her sister a sidewise glance as if to remind her of the warning note. Since neither of them had told Miss Parker about it, the teacher headed the car in the direction of the Crossroads Inn. Reaching it, she looked at her wrist watch, then said eagerly:

"I didn't have a chance to investigate the historic old building the other day. Maybe we could spare a few minutes now to look around."

The Danas were delighted at the suggestion. Excitedly they took the flashlight from the glove compartment and led the way on foot through the tangled undergrowth to the Civil War inn.

Suddenly Louise stared fixedly at a nearby tree. She called the others' attention to a piece of green cloth which fluttered from one of the lower branches. Wondering why it was there, she climbed up to retrieve it.

"Why, it's a kerchief," she reported.

She dropped the square of silk down to Jean and slid to the ground.

"There's writing on this kerchief!" Jean said excitedly. "But I don't understand it."

"I believe it's written in the Romany language," Miss Parker spoke up, after studying the words.

"Maybe it's one of Nura's kerchiefs," Jean suggested. "She might have left a message for someone."

"Her sweetheart, Stivo, perhaps," Louise guessed. "I wonder what *cirikle* means?"

"I haven't the slightest idea," the teacher admitted. "It's possible that some other gypsy left this for Nura."

At once Louise wondered if the message had anything to do with Nura's message that there was danger at the crossroads. She might be in such difficulty that she hesitated to ask the Danas for any further assistance.

"In that case, we should bend every effort to help

her," Louise told herself. Tying the kerchief around her neck in a loose knot, she said aloud, "Why don't we take this along and have it translated by the gyspies?"

"I think that's an excellent idea," Miss Parker said. "Perhaps we shouldn't delay here any longer. I'll investigate the interior of the inn another time."

The three were about to move off when they heard a muffled cry from the old building.

Jean stiffened. "That might have come from Nura," she said tensely. "The poor girl may be a prisoner!"

With only one thought in mind—that of rescue—the Danas and their companion rushed for the porch.

Louise pulled at the loose board which the girls had removed once before.

"Be careful," Miss Parker warned anxiously as Louise stepped sideways over the sill.

As her foot sought the floor of the dark lobby, and before she had a chance to snap on the flashlight, Louise suddenly felt the touch of an icy hand on the back of her neck. Terrified, she jerked backward to the porch.

"What's the matter?" Jean asked, seeing her sister's blanched face.

Louise was so startled that for an instant she could not reply. Then, grabbing her throat, she realized that the green kerchief was gone!

CHAPTER XII

A Worried Musician

"THE kerchief!" Louise gasped. "It was pulled right off my neck!"

"What!" Jean cried, now noting that it was missing. "Did you see who took it?"

"No. I'll find out, though!" Louise said with determination.

"No! No!" Miss Parker protested, seizing Louise's arm. "I cannot permit you to go into that building. It's entirely too risky."

"I hate to lose the kerchief. The writing on it may mean a great deal in helping Nura," Louise persisted.

"We must go for the police," the teacher decided. "This is a matter for them to handle."

Louise and Jean knew that Miss Parker's advice was sound. Nevertheless, they were reluctant to leave the inn, fearing that by the time they returned with the authorities, the intruder would be gone.

"Suppose two of us remain here to keep watch," Jean suggested.

"No, indeed." The teacher shook her head. "We must stick together."

The three started for the car. Midway to the road, they heard someone crashing through the brush toward them. The person who emerged from the woods was a handsome young man, whistling a gay dance tune. They noticed that he carried a violin.

Presently he found himself face to face with the Danas and their chaperone. He was olive-skinned and black-eyed, and wore a red sash beneath his jacket. They wondered if he were a gypsy.

With a very engaging smile he said, "Good afternoon. Splendid day, isn't it? By any chance, have you seen a gypsy girl in the woods?"

"Is her name Nura?" Louise asked, making a shrewd guess.

"Yes! You know her? You have seen her?"

"We know her, but we haven't met her here today," Louise answered. "Are you her friend Stivo?"

The young man could not hide his astonishment. "You know my name?"

"Nura told us about you," Louise explained.

"You are her friends. Then you are mine also!" A warm glow spread over the young man's smooth-shaven face. It was followed by a slightly sad expression.

"I had hoped to see Nura here. But at least she promised to leave a message for me," the man revealed.

"I must search for it. *Te tres!* Long life to you!"

He started to move on. Louise, however, stopped him. "Could Nura's message have been written on a kerchief?" she queried.

Stivo whirled around, his eyes dancing. "Yes, yes!" he cried. "Do you know where the kerchief is?"

Regretfully Louise told him how she had discovered it, only to have the kerchief snatched away by someone lurking inside the inn.

The information dismayed Stivo. "That kerchief was meant for me—only me! No one must see the message! If it should fall into the wrong hands, Nura may be harmed!"

Louise was aghast. She felt responsible for the kerchief's loss and wished she had left it in the tree.

"I'm dreadfully sorry," she said. "Perhaps the person who snatched it may still be inside the inn."

"I'll get him!" Stivo cried. "Hold my violin, will you, please?"

Handing it to Miss Parker, he darted off toward the inn. Uncertain as to what might happen, the Danas and the teacher followed him. By the time they reached the dilapidated old structure, Stivo was out of sight. As they waited anxiously, he suddenly climbed out the front window of the inn.

"Did you get the kerchief?" Jean asked him eagerly.

Stivo shook his head in disgust. "The place is empty, so far as I could see. It was pretty dark inside."

"Too bad," Louise commented. "Someone certainly was in there ten minutes ago." She looked at Miss Parker. "If no one is in the inn, this would be an ideal time to investigate. We might find a clue."

"Stivo is here to protect us," Jean said as the teacher hesitated.

"I guess it will be safe enough," Miss Parker consented, but with reluctance.

She followed Stivo, Jean, and Louise into the dark interior. While Louise held the flashlight, the gypsy, sure-footed as a cat, moved rapidly from room to room over the creaky boards on the first and second floors. All the group were disappointed not to find the kerchief and were sure that it had been taken away.

"This certainly is a fascinating place," Miss Parker remarked as they started for the stairs. "But I wouldn't want to stay here as Nura has been doing."

Jean was about to reply when she kicked a small, soft object on the floor. Wondering what it might be, she leaned down to pick it up.

"A leather wallet!" she exclaimed.

Excited by the discovery, Jean requested her sister to bring the flashlight closer.

"Anything in it?"

"No. O-oh!" Jean squealed in amazement as she saw a driver's license inside. "This is Professor Crandall's lost wallet!"

Louise gasped and Miss Parker looked puzzled. The sisters quickly explained.

"But how did it get here?" the teacher asked.

"It must have been stolen," Louise replied. "He said it had at least fifty dollars in it."

Finding the wallet gave the sisters another idea. Maybe the missing notes were here too!

Again a search began, with Stivo helping. But the professor's lost papers could not be found. And Louise and Jean did not come upon a single clue to indicate who might have dropped the empty wallet.

"This is very baffling!" Miss Parker said.

Stivo could cast no light upon the mystery. He had not seen Nura since she had come to the inn, and knew nothing of what had been going on.

During the conversation, Jean told him about finding the antique silver spoon and described the piece with the bearded man's head at the top of the handle.

"Oddly enough, it disappeared too," she said. "Stivo, do you know if anyone in your tribe owned such a spoon?"

"No, I have never seen one like that." Then, eager to leave, he took his violin, saying, "I must continue my hunt for Nura. I have a good job now and can support her in gajo style. As soon as I find her, we will be married."

"Without King Sando's consent?" Jean asked.

Stivo looked very solemn. "He does not understand our love."

"Old gypsy customs," said Miss Parker kindly, "and today's ways in America differ greatly. I suppose you young people have to make a choice."

"Do you mean Nura may have changed her mind?" Stivo asked quickly. "No, no, she would not do that. More likely Zarka, the man her father has chosen to be her husband, traced her here. The message on the scarf probably told where Nura has gone into hiding."

The Danas were fearful that the person who had snatched the scarf was Zarka, but they did not mention it. Now he would find Nura in her new hiding place!

But Stivo read their thoughts. "If I find Zarka," he said, his handsome face darkening, "I will attend to him in true gypsy fashion."

Stivo did not explain, but his listeners knew that a gypsy never forgot a wrong any more than he did a kind deed. Abruptly the young violinist changed the subject. He told them of his wonderful plans for his and Nura's future.

"I play the violin at the Rose Tree Restaurant in Harkness," he said. "Sometimes I fill in as a gypsy solo dancer."

"How interesting!" Miss Parker remarked.

Louise's eyes sparkled. "Jean and I must go there sometime to hear you."

"Please come," he invited them. "And if you should get any word from my Nura, you will let me know at once, won't you?"

"Yes, indeed," Louise assured him. "And that may be sooner than you think. We're on our way to your people's camp at Franklyn. Nura told us to contact Sebenca."

Stivo was surprised to hear this. "To have your fortunes told?" he asked.

"Oh, no," Jean answered quickly. "We promised to try locating the stolen skafidi so that—"

As Jean hesitated, the gypsy grabbed her hand and said excitedly, "To clear my name? To give me a chance to go back to my tribe? You are true friends. I will never forget you."

Jean was embarrassed by his effusiveness and merely nodded, smiling. Stivo, realizing this, dropped her hand.

"The gypsy camp is well hidden," he said. "Do you know how to find it?"

"Not exactly."

"I will draw you a rough map," the gypsy offered.

He took a restaurant menu from his jacket pocket, and with a stubby pencil, began to draw on the back of it.

As the girls watched, fascinated, he sketched in a small rippling brook, several tall trees, and many odd little marks that they suddenly realized were tents.

"Here is the main road," he said, drawing rapidly, "and here is the path you must follow. You'll climb a hill and there will be the camp! But you'll have to look sharp or you'll miss it."

He handed the map to Louise. "When you see Sebenca tell her that Stivo sends a kiss," he requested. "In secret, give her word that I have a good job and await Nura."

"We surely will," Louise promised. "And if we see Nura, we'll send her to you."

Stivo smiled, a look of deep gratitude in his eyes. "You are good gajos," he said quietly. "I will remember."

He started away. "God go with you," he added in farewell. "We will meet again."

CHAPTER XIII

The Hidden Camp

AFTER leaving Stivo, the Danas drove nearly ten miles with Miss Parker to a wooded section beyond the town of Franklyn. Parking the car in an inconspicuous place, they set off to find the gypsy camp.

For nearly fifteen minutes, the trio wandered along the trail indicated on Stivo's map, seeking the caravan, but in vain.

"Girls, do you think we could have taken the wrong trail?" Miss Parker murmured worriedly.

"Oh, I don't think so," Louise reassured her. "Stivo warned us that the camp was well hidden."

A little farther on, the three rounded a hill and suddenly caught their first glimpse of the encampment. Tents were pitched in parallel lines on a low, wooded knoll by a brook.

In the midst of the camp a great fire roared. From the aroma the callers guessed that a meat stew was cooking in an iron pot which hung above the blaze. An elderly woman in a red-and-yellow costume squatted nearby, waiting to stir the concoction when necessary.

"I hope that there won't be any trouble when we announce ourselves," Miss Parker said nervously. "Romanies are friendly, I know. Even so, I feel uneasy about the feud which apparently has developed between Stivo and Zarka."

"No one knows of our interest in Nura," Louise pointed out. "We'll pretend we're just casual visitors until we find Sebenca."

Moving closer, the visitors could hear laughter and the barking of dogs. Someone was playing a violin.

"They seem happy," Louise remarked. "Much happier than Nura."

Miss Parker called the attention of her companions to the tents. "Notice that they all face south," she said. "A gypsy will never tell you why, but I suspect it is because the south side is the warmest in winter."

The three approached the camp with a show of confidence. Miss Parker nearly lost her courage, however, as a pack of barking dogs surrounded them. But the animals made no move to attack.

A stout man in high boots strode quickly to meet the callers. The Danas thought that he was the same gypsy whose car had nearly struck the school's station wagon.

"*Katar aves, prala?*" he inquired. "Whence come you?"

Miss Parker politely explained that her young friends had a great desire to visit a gypsy camp.

"You are welcome," he responded politely.

The man raised his hand in a signal, and immediately the visitors were surrounded by a swarm of laughing, chattering children.

"Aren't they darling!" Jean cried, admiring their bright eyes and rosy cheeks.

Miss Parker and the sisters wandered deeper into the camp. Several gypsy women approached them, offering to tell their fortunes. The younger ones were pretty and wore bright-hued, ankle-length skirts heavily ornamented with bangles. Gold-coin necklaces hung about their necks. The middle-aged wives were less gaily dressed and none of them wore shoes.

The very old women were unattractive and bent from years of hard labor. One, who from her appearance might have been a witch, bestowed a toothless grin upon the visitors as they passed her tent.

A young girl sidled up to Louise and smiled. "Tell your fortune?" she coaxed.

"Not unless your name is Sebenca," Louise replied.

"You want Sebenca?" the gypsy asked, her dark eyes widening in surprise.

"We met a man named Stivo—" Miss Parker blurted out, much to the Danas' dismay.

"Stivo—" The gypsy girl darted a quick glance toward a large tent that stood at one side of the camp. In a hushed voice she murmured, "You must not speak his name aloud. King Sando may hear you! Where is Stivo?"

The sisters knew better than to reveal the young man's whereabouts. Louise merely said, "Please take us to Sebenca."

The gypsy shrugged and motioned for the three to follow her. She led them to a large wooden van set back among the trees.

"While you're talking to Sebenca," the history teacher said, "suppose I chat with some of the other gypsies. I want to learn about the origin of this tribe and some of its customs."

After Miss Parker had turned away, the gypsy girl thrust her head through the open van door. She spoke rapidly in her own tongue to the old woman inside. Then she told the Dana girls that they might enter.

Sebenca, deeply wrinkled and stooped, raised up from a crouching position beside a built-in bed at the far end of the van. Beside it a wooden table hung by hinges from the wall.

Sebenca smiled at the visitors. "Stivo sent you?" she muttered.

"Not exactly. Nura did," Jean replied. "She was going to tell you about our coming."

"I haven't seen her. But you are welcome," Sebenca replied.

"We are here because we want to help both Stivo and Nura," Louise spoke up.

"This is not a trick? You are not friends of Zarka?"

"Oh, no!" Louise assured her.

The old woman rose and closed the van door.

"Now we can talk without unfriendly ears drinking in our words," she said. "You have a message from Stivo?"

"He sent you a kiss," Louise told her. "And he said he is working at the Rose Tree Restaurant in Harkness. Stivo is very much upset because Nura has run away again. Do you know where she might be?"

A startled expression came over Sebenca's face. She motioned the girls to take seats on feather cushions which served as chairs, then said, "Nura has not been back here since she went away. Because of Sando, she dared not come."

Lost in deep thought, the old woman stared straight ahead.

"Why does King Sando oppose Nura's marriage to Stivo?" Louise asked.

Sebenca's eyes blazed. "Sando was bought by Zarka's gold!"

"Where did he obtain it?" Louise pursued the subject. "By hard work?"

Sebenca made a hissing sound through her teeth. "Zarka work! He is lazy! He lies all day in the sun, boasting of his horse-trading deals! How would Zarka get riches except by one way? He stole the money!"

The Danas were excited by this information. "You know that to be so, Sebenca?" Jean asked.

The old gypsy nodded. "I do not have proof. But here"—she pounded her heart—"Sebenca knows!"

Prompted by skillful questions from Louise and Jean the old fortuneteller disclosed that a very tense situation had developed in camp. The gypsies were taking sides, some with Zarka and others with Stivo. King Sando himself blamed the unrest upon the friendliness of the young people with non-gypsies.

"Nura and Stivo both went to gajo school," Sebenca disclosed. "They began to question gypsy ways and customs. Nura and Stivo fell in love, but Zarka also wanted her. So he offered gold for her, and King Sando says he is a worthy suitor."

Louise asked the views of Nura's mother regarding such a marriage.

"Jiva—she sides with Nura," Sebenca answered. "But even she cannot oppose King Sando. His word is law here."

By this time, the sisters were convinced that the old fortuneteller could be trusted completely. Accordingly, Louise told how they had become acquainted with Nura and why they had promised to try finding the stolen silver tray. Then she mentioned the kerchief with the gypsy writing on it and how it had been snatched from her neck.

"If we had been able to read the words, we might have learned where Nura went," Louise said regretfully.

Sebenca asked the girls if they could recall any of the words on the scarf.

"I remember one," Louise said at once. "It was cirikle."

"That means bird," the fortuneteller translated.

"Wasn't one of the words *kris*?" Jean asked, thinking hard. "I'm sure it was."

"Kris is our word for tribunal," Sebenca said, becoming excited. "What were some of the others?"

"*Tsera*," Louise repeated after long thought. "Or is that a word?"

"Yes, it means tent! Nura may have written that she wants to return to the tribe and let the Council hold a trial!"

"She could do that?" Louise questioned in surprise.

Sebenca nodded. "Even a king can be exiled from his tribe if the Council decides he has wronged his people. Trials are held, too, if a husband or wife is accused of leaving camp with the family money."

"Then if the Council votes against Zarka, Nura would be allowed to marry Stivo?" Louise asked excitedly.

"Yes. But King Sando is cunning. He is set against the marriage. If he learns that Nura is asking for a trial, he will try to prevent it."

"He won't hear it from us," Louise said. "But the person who took the scarf may tell him."

"For once Sebenca is not able to see the future," the old woman said sadly.

"I think we should leave," Jean urged. "Miss Parker will be looking for us. Anyway, if we stay with Sebenca too long, Louise, it may arouse Sando's suspicions."

Louise agreed. Before saying good-by to the fortuneteller, the girls promised that if they solved the mystery of the silver tray, they would communicate with her. Sebenca, in turn, said she would try to get in touch with the Danas if she had any news.

"We may break camp at any hour," the old gypsy said. "Sando is restless. Zarka keeps urging him to move southward."

"Then be sure to tell us where you go," Louise begged her.

"I will not forget," the old woman promised.

The girls said good-by and went off to look for Miss Parker. The sisters found the history teacher talking to Jiva, queen of the gypsies. She was middle-aged and very beautiful. Nura looked very much like her mother and they both had the same sweet, sad expression in their eyes. The sisters wanted to reveal their secret to her but decided it would be best not to.

Miss Parker introduced them and added excitedly, "I've been learning so many fascinating things about this tribe and their language! They came from England many years ago. The members have been in a dozen countries and in nearly every part of the United States!"

"Did you learn any words in the language?" Jean asked.

"I wish I'd had the time! Jiva tells me that the English gypsies call their language Romanes. It consists of some three thousand words, many of Indian or Sanskrit origin. The language has few verbs."

"Did Jiva tell you about any interesting customs?" Louise asked.

"Yes. She said that sometimes a wooden ring is sent to a gypsy to summon him to a secret trial for his life."

The Danas were eager to question Jiva about gypsy marriage customs. But before they could do so, the gypsy queen was called away by the angry voice of an unseen man. Without explanation, she vanished into one of the tents.

"It looks as if someone ordered her not to talk to us!" Jean commented.

"The gypsies seem to be watching us rather suspiciously now," Louise added in an undertone, as she saw them going into their tents one by one.

"I can't understand the quick change of attitude,"

Miss Parker remarked nervously. "Everyone was friendly at first. Jiva answered all of my questions. She told me that the gypsies originated in India and from that country wandered all over the world."

"I have a feeling that they've seen our car," said Louise. "They may think we've come to make trouble because of that gypsy who nearly hit us at the crossroads when we were with Professor Crandall."

"Or someone may have overheard our conversation with Sebenca," Jean said.

"We'd better go quickly," Miss Parker urged.

As the three reached the edge of the camp, two gypsy men overtook them. Without warning, the Danas and Miss Parker were seized by their arms.

The teacher tried to pull away. "Let us go!" she cried. "What is the meaning of this?"

She could not free herself. And Louise and Jean, held firmly by their grim-lipped gypsy captors, were powerless.

Offering no explanation, the men shoved their three visitors to the largest tent in camp. The Danas guessed instantly that King Sando had sent for them.

With fast-beating hearts, they steeled themselves for an unpleasant scene.

CHAPTER XIV

King Sando

THE gypsy leader, a stout red-faced man with a stern expression, gazed at Louise, Jean, and Miss Parker from a couch of pillows on which he was reclining. He arose with difficulty as the three were shoved in front of him.

Glancing around quickly, the girls saw a younger man in the background, leaning indolently against the tent pole. His lips were drawn into a triumphant grin.

"They are the ones," he said.

Instantly Louise recognized him as the second reckless gypsy driver near the Crossroads Inn.

"Why have we been brought here?" Miss Parker demanded indignantly. "I insist that you let us go."

"You speak to Sando, king of the gypsies!" one of their captors flared up.

"We appreciate the honor," the teacher responded sarcastically. "Nevertheless, it is late and we must return to Starhurst School."

Sando fixed his three visitors with a glittering eye. "You will leave only when you tell me what you have done with my daughter Nura."

The Danas gasped. "We?" they said, and Louise added, "We have no idea what became of her."

"You lie! Zarka"—the king waved toward the young man with the triumphant smile—"heard you talking to Sebenca in the van!"

Louise and Jean exchanged quick glances. The young gypsy who eyed them so insolently had been eavesdropping!

How much had he learned? Not a great deal, they reasoned. When talking to the old fortuneteller, they had kept their voices very low.

"We've met your daughter, King Sando, and like her very much," Louise said. "Nura told us about this camp, so, being curious, we decided to visit you. Evidently we're not welcome."

The suggestion that gypsies were not hospitable irked King Sando.

"You are welcome here if you come as friends," he replied stiffly. "But I will not allow meddling! Where are you hiding Nura?"

Miss Parker stepped forward. "This is a ridiculous accusation. We are not hiding Nura, and we don't know where she is. Now we'll go!"

Zarka bounded to the king's side. "We should complain to the police," he muttered in the gypsy ruler's ear.

"I wouldn't do that if I were in your place," Miss Parker spoke up quickly. "If the police become interested in Nura's disappearance they'll ask *you* plenty of questions, too."

The teacher's statement seemed to frighten Sando. Dropping his arrogant manner, he said:

"You are speaking the truth in saying you are not hiding my daughter?"

"We are," Louise responded.

"Then go!" the gypsy king suddenly ordered with a wave of his bejeweled fingers.

As the callers walked hurriedly away they could hear Zarka arguing with Sando. He was evidently trying to convince Sando that the Danas knew where Nura was, but they did not hear the king's answer.

Not until the three reached the station wagon did Miss Parker breathe easily. "Whew! What an experience!" she exclaimed, sliding into the driver's seat. "I learned a great deal about gypsies today—almost too much!"

"Let's take the longer route back to Starhurst School," Louise suggested as the teacher turned the car around.

"I had intended to go by way of the crossroads," she said. "It's shorter."

"We may be followed," Louise commented. "I don't trust that Zarka."

"I never thought of that! You're right, Louise. I'll take the other road."

It was fortunate that she selected the main, well-traveled highway. Within ten minutes after leaving the gypsy camp, Louise called her attention to a familiar car that trailed them at a speed which exactly matched their own.

"Zarka is checking up on us," she remarked.

"We'll fool him!" Jean declared. "Step on it, Miss Parker!"

Not until they entered the town of Penfield did they lose the gypsy car. A block from Starhurst School it turned off onto a side street.

"I hope we convinced that awful creature we weren't going to the inn," Jean chuckled, "or any other place where we might be hiding Nura."

Alighting at the garage, the Danas were amazed to see Lettie Briggs strolling through the grounds with Professor Stanley. She had locked arms with him and the two seemed to be on very friendly terms.

"Lettie seems to have made a conquest!" Jean said with an amused chuckle. "Well, she's welcome to her 'dream' man!"

The others laughed and went into the dormitory. At dinner the Danas discovered that the school was abuzz with gossip about Lettie. The foolish girl, flattered by the professor's attention, had boasted to everyone that he was "crazy" about her.

"He's crazy all right," Evelyn Starr declared to Louise and Jean. "How he can listen to Lettie's chatter is a mystery to me!"

"He doesn't seem to mind," Louise said thoughtfully.

"They've talked a lot," Evelyn reported. "I saw them together several times today."

"Lettie may be trying to interest him in some of her wild schemes," Jean remarked. "You know she said she was going to solve a mystery."

A lecture which Professor Stanley had been scheduled to deliver that night was canceled at the last minute by Mrs. Crandall. Since no explanation was offered for the change of program, the sisters wondered what had happened.

The free social hour, however, was greatly welcomed by the students. Jean and Louise used the time to return to Professor Crandall the empty wallet they had recovered that afternoon.

"Where did you find it?" he asked in amazement.

"At the Crossroads Inn," replied Louise.

"But I was never in that building!"

"Someone dropped the wallet there after taking out the money," Jean told him, "but maybe it wasn't dropped on purpose. The person may have been hiding there."

Suddenly a sickening thought came to the girls. The inn had been Nura's hiding place and she had visited Starhurst. It was possible that she had stolen the wallet and then deliberately told the sisters to stay away from the old hotel! Before they had a chance to voice their thoughts, Professor Crandall asked:

"You didn't find my notes too?"

"No," Louise said. "But tomorrow Jean and I will search in all your favorite haunts on the campus. Your papers may turn up somewhere."

"I certainly hope so." The professor sighed.

"Six months' work will be wasted if I fail to recover them. It makes me fairly ill to think of the loss."

True to their promise, the Dana girls made another search the following day. They visited the museum, library, various classrooms, and the summerhouse, but to no avail. The missing notes were not in any of them.

"Where on earth could Professor Crandall have put them?" Jean pondered as they entered the school gym.

"It's certainly strange that we haven't found them," Louise admitted. "I'm beginning to think perhaps someone did take them. But what would be the purpose of it?"

"Well, let's not worry about it now," Jean said, opening her locker and taking out her tennis clothes. "You know, I need some new socks. These poor things have seen better days!"

An intensive workout on the courts kept the Danas

from any more sleuthing on the gypsy mystery. And there was no lecture that evening, either.

Early the next morning Evelyn Starr came rushing excitedly into their study. She waved a newspaper before their eyes.

"Read this!" she said. "Here are two items that will amaze you!"

Evelyn spread the front page of the *Franklyn Morning Star* on Jean's desk. She pointed to a three-paragraph item from the town of Westerville.

The news story stated that gypsies near that town had reported to the police the previous day the theft of several pieces of ancient jewelry and one of their valuable skafidis. The king of the tribe had declared no gypsy would steal such things from another and that the thief must be a gajo. The chief of police had stated that a theft from gypsies by a gajo was unheard of.

"What a mix-up!" Louise said. "I wonder if the thief could be the same one who stole the silver tray from Nura's tribe."

"Well, listen to this!" Evelyn went on.

A second item in the paper gave a brief account of a jewelry-store robbery in Franklyn. An unusual aspect of the crime was that only antique jewelry had been stolen. Many modern pieces of value had been overlooked, apparently with deliberate intent.

"That is strange," said Louise.

"It sounds as if the two stories tie together!" Jean exclaimed.

"With one exception," said Evelyn, reading on. " 'Police reported finding several clues which indicate that the thief may be a gypsy. Chief Brady immediately ordered a search of the Romany encampment near here.' "

"King Sando's tribe!" Louise cried. "What did they find out?"

Evelyn read the next sentence dramatically.

" 'When police reached the gypsy camp last night they found it deserted.' "

"Deserted!" the Danas exclaimed.

" 'So far the police have not been able to trace them,' " Evelyn went on.

"I wonder if Sebenca will send us word," Louise said thoughtfully.

CHAPTER XV

The Investigation

"If the police are after King Sando's tribe," said Evelyn, "you'll probably never hear from Sebenca."

Louise carefully reread the newspaper accounts of the theft. "If the gypsies are innocent, they may not even know that the police are after them," she commented thoughtfully.

"That's the way it strikes me, too," Jean agreed. "Anyway, I've been told that gypsies seldom, if ever, go beyond petty thievery. Picking pockets is more in their line than breaking and entering a jewelry store to take antique silver."

"The gypsies may have broken camp for an entirely different reason," Louise commented. "For that matter, Sebenca told us that the tribe might move at any time, remember?"

"That's right," Jean replied. "Then if the gypsies

115

didn't break into the jewelry store, someone must have planted those clues to make it look that way."

"How about Zarka?" Evelyn suggested. "You said he is suspected of having stolen from his own tribe."

The Danas had to admit this was true.

"But we're only speculating," Louise remarked. "What I'd like is more information. These newspaper accounts are pretty skimpy."

Evelyn suggested that the girls contact the Penfield police. She pointed out that they surely would know about the case.

"That's a good idea," Jean approved. "But I wonder if they'd tell us what we want to know."

"Oh, you and Louise are well acquainted with Chief Riley," Evelyn said. "You've given him some clues on several occasions."

"Yes," Louise replied. "I guess he'll do it."

"And we can report how we found Professor Crandall's empty wallet at the Crossroads Inn," Jean added. "Let's go right away. We'll ask the old darling to drive us there before his first class."

The Danas received permission from the headmistress to make the trip directly after breakfast.

Since the day was a little cool, the girls returned to their rooms for sweaters.

"Louise," Jean said, gazing at the clothes in her closet. "Do you think we should wear suits and perhaps dress up a little for the trip?"

"What for?" Louise asked. "We'll be coming right back in time for classes."

"Yes, you're right." Jean sighed. "But that new lilac suit of mine looks so neglected. I've had it more than a week and still haven't worn it!"

"It will keep," Louise said, laughing. "Here's your pink sweater. Now come on, or we'll be late in getting back."

The sisters met Professor Crandall at the garage.

"I wish one of you girls would drive," he said. "Louise, you have a license, haven't you? I've been so nervous the last few days that I can't keep my wits about me. I think constantly of my lost notes—what *could* I have done with them?"

"Don't give up hope, Professor Crandall," Louise said kindly. "They'll be sure to turn up soon."

The elderly man shook his head. "It may be too late. I am to present a lecture next week before the Philosophical Association in Atlanta. Unless I recover my papers before that time, I must cancel the speech."

"Oh, that's a shame," the girls chorused, and determined to make another attempt to help him locate his notes.

Louise and Jean had told no one except Evelyn and Doris of their destination. But Lettie and Ina, who witnessed their departure, were consumed with curiosity and tried without success to learn where the girls had gone.

"They're up to something," Evelyn heard Lettie confide to her roommate. "I'll have to watch them closer in the future!"

"That might be easier if you didn't stick so close to Professor Stanley!" Ina retorted maliciously. "You go for walks with him every chance you get. He's taking all of your attention."

"You mind your own business, Ina Mason!" Lettie snapped. "I'll pay as much attention as I please to Professor Stanley! He admires me very much."

Ina's reply was a snickering laugh which further angered her friend, who stumped off huffily.

Meanwhile, in Penfield, Louise, Jean, and Professor Crandall had entered Police Chief Riley's office. He shook hands with the teacher and greeted the Dana girls warmly.

"Well! Well!" he beamed, waving them into chairs. "What is it this time, girls? A mystery? Arson? Grand larceny?"

The sisters laughed, but Professor Crandall looked a trifle shocked.

"Only a theft to report," Louise replied, and told the chief about the professor's wallet.

The officer gave the professor a lengthy report to fill out, saying, "We'll do what we can to recover your money. But, frankly, I doubt that you'll get it back. The clues are too slim."

"Jean and I thought it might help to know that the

wallet was recovered at the old Crossroads Inn,"
Louise remarked in disappointment.

"It's helpful," Chief Riley admitted, "but unless
the thief left some mark or item that was distinctive,
our chances of finding him seem pretty hopeless."

Jean had brought along the newspaper clipping
about the jewelry-store theft in Franklyn. She revealed that the sisters thought there might be a connection between the stolen wallet and the missing antique
jewelry.

"Could you give us more detailed information?"
she asked.

"We've paid only routine attention to the case
here," the chief answered. "But if you're interested,
I'll call Franklyn and find out more about it."

"Oh, would you, please?" Jean urged eagerly.

"We especially want to know," said Louise, "what
the clues are that made them think gypsies broke into
the store."

"I'll phone right away," Chief Riley said, dialing
the number.

Within ten minutes he had obtained the information
which the girls desired. Hanging up, he relayed it to
the Danas.

"The Franklyn police chief tells me that he's convinced gypsies were involved, because of one special
clue."

"What is it?" Jean asked excitedly.

"The chief thinks that the thief may have been a girl. Or possibly a girl served as an accomplice. Detectives found a kerchief with Romany words on it. The scarf was dropped on the floor of the jewelry store."

"A green scarf?" Louise asked quickly, thinking instantly of the one which had been snatched from her neck at the Crossroads Inn.

"That's right. How did you know about it?"

"And the Romany words on it—were they words such as cirikle or tsera perhaps?" Louise added, without answering his question.

Police Chief Riley stared. "Say, how did you know that?" he demanded. "You know more about this case than you're letting on."

"We don't actually know very much," Louise said modestly. "We have a theory, though, that the kerchief was deliberately planted in the jewelry store. Either that, or it was dropped accidentally by the person who snatched it from me at the old inn."

She then went on to tell how she had found the kerchief and how it had been jerked from her neck.

"Do you know who did this?" the captain asked hopefully.

Louise shook her head. Secretly she was fearful that the person might have been Nura. One suspicion after another seemed to be piling up against the gypsy girl! The thought made Louise heartsick. Nura had seemed so innocent and so lovely.

"Jean and I started out to help her and now we're condemning her, and without a shred of proof!" Louise chided herself.

"This is mighty interesting information," the officer said. "I'll pass it on to the Franklyn police right away."

"Chief Riley, what police check the Crossroads Inn?" Jean asked him suddenly.

"Not my men," he replied. "That territory belongs to the state troopers. Why?"

"They make routine checkups?"

"Oh, once in a great while. Say, young lady, what's on your mind?"

Jean told the chief about Nura being ordered out of the old inn and warned to stay away.

"She said it was a policeman who drove her out."

"When was this?"

"Three days ago."

"I'll check at once."

This time Chief Riley telephoned the state police headquarters for that vicinity. He was told none of the troopers had been to the old inn on that day.

"Then the policeman must have been a phony!" Jean cried upon hearing the report.

"He certainly was," the chief grunted. "*H-m*, if someone is impersonating the police, we'll get right after him!" He jotted down a few notes on a pad. "Now, what about this gypsy girl you saw there? Where can we find her?"

The Danas said that they did not know—she was a member of the tribe that had vanished.

"Do you think this scarf belonged to her?" the officer asked.

"We don't know that, either," Jean answered.

"But you feel that the scarf was only a plant to throw suspicion on the girl or her tribe?"

"Yes," Jean said, after a warning look from Louise. "So even if the owner were traced, that person might not be the real thief!"

The chief smiled. "In your own way, you girls have certainly come to the defense of this gypsy girl. Well, I hope you're right."

Suddenly Louise leaned forward in her chair. Earnestly she said:

"Chief Riley, I don't want to interfere with police methods, but I think if you could catch that phony policeman, you'd solve the mystery."

The officer slapped his desk. "I'm going to follow your advice and set a trap for him at once. He may be using the Crossroads Inn as a hide-out."

CHAPTER XVI

A Double Warning

THE next day, the Dana girls waited hopefully for word from Chief Riley about the fake policeman who might be connected with the mystery of the crossroads. Late in the afternoon they received a telephone call from him.

Jean answered. The state police, he said, had searched the inn but had found no one there. Moreover, none of the missing loot had been secreted in it so far as the officers could discover.

"Well, what's our next move, Louise?" Jean asked as she left the phone booth.

"I wish we could trace the gypsy tribe."

"Big order." Jean laughed, and added hopefully, "Maybe we'll hear from Sebenca or Nura."

"It's nerve-racking, though, just to wait." Louise sighed. "In the meantime, let's look further for Professor Crandall's notes."

123

This time the girls searched through piles of old newspapers and magazines in the cellar of the school, but the missing research material was not among them. During the early evening the sisters attended another lecture by Professor Stanley. The man was a poor speaker, and his talk on historical landmarks in the United States was not well organized. Many students slipped out of the auditorium before he finished. Louise and Jean, though bored, remained until the end.

"Wasn't he simply magnificent?" Lettie drooled. She had sat in the front row, with the Danas directly back of her. "Such a wealth of knowledge!" she said pompously.

The sisters made no comment. They went forward to ask the lecturer a few questions. To them the answers were not very clear and Jean changed the subject.

"Have you visited the Civil War inn at the crossroads?"

"Yes, I have," the professor replied. "I'll never go back there again, though."

"Why?" Jean asked in surprise. "Didn't you find it interesting?"

"It's a dangerous wreck. Any sensible person would avoid the place. You know, of course, that the last owners of the inn and most of their unfortunate guests died of smallpox."

"Why, no!" Louise exclaimed.

"The place should be avoided like poison."

"Surely after all these years a building couldn't remain germ infested," Jean protested.

"That's where you're wrong," Professor Stanley returned. "Aside from the smallpox danger, the floor is caving in. Under the rotted boards are deep wells. To fall into one of them would mean certain drowning."

During this speech Lettie turned to the Danas, a smirk on her face.

"I hope you'll take the advice," she remarked loftily.

Doris Harland, who had joined the group in time to hear the lecturer's warning, was aghast to hear about the inn.

"You girls must never go to that dreadful place again!" she admonished Louise and Jean.

"That's sound advice," agreed Professor Stanley. "Stay away from the inn, and tell all the other students and your teachers to do likewise."

He turned abruptly and left the auditorium.

"When do you suppose Professor Stanley visited the inn?" Jean speculated. "I would have asked him, but he walked away."

"Please take his advice and don't go there again," Doris pleaded. "How horrible if you should get smallpox!"

"That part of the story sounds ridiculous," Jean said.

"You might fall through the floor into one of those wells!" Doris said fearfully.

"That part has me worried," Louise admitted reluctantly. "It's a fact that the flooring is in bad condition. And what's in the cellar, we don't know, of course."

"I'll bet Professor Stanley was exaggerating," Jean spoke up. "Why should a hotel be built with a lot of wells in the cellar? If there was that much water around, the builders would have chosen another spot."

"What I can't understand," said Doris, "is why Professor Stanley went to the inn himself."

"It's interesting historically," Louise suggested. "Speaking of history, do you girls recall Mrs. Henrietta Parsons?"

"That nice old lady who lives at the edge of Penfield?" Doris asked.

"Yes. Mrs. Crandall often invites her to tea. She's one of Penfield's oldest inhabitants and is considered an authority on local history."

"She should know all about the inn, then!"

"That was what I was thinking, Jean. Why not call on her tomorrow and check the story?"

"Fine!" Jean approved. "I'll ask Mrs. Crandall for permission."

She received it, and the following afternoon the Danas went to see her. Mrs. Parsons looked charmingly old-fashioned in a pale-blue dress edged with lace around the neck. After admiring her collection of old china, the sisters broached the subject of the Crossroads Inn.

"Is it true that the owner and many guests died of smallpox?" Louise asked.

"If they did, I never heard of it," Mrs. Parsons replied. "The inn had several owners. The last one just couldn't make the place pay. When I was a girl, the building was nicely kept up. Now I'm told that it is falling into ruin."

"It is," Louise said. "The floors are rotting away. Jean and I have been warned not to go there because we might tumble through to the wells in the cellar."

"Wells? What do you mean, my dear?"

"We were told there are a number of them—deep wells in which we could drown."

"Whoever gave you such information?"

"Professor Stanley."

"And who is he, pray?"

"A lecturer at the school," Louise explained. "Actually, we don't know much about him."

"I hesitate to contradict your professor," Mrs. Parsons said, "but I'm sure I don't know where he heard such a story."

"Then it's not true about the wells?" Jean asked quickly.

"I certainly never heard of them."

"The inn really isn't so dangerous then?"

"As to that, I can't say," Mrs. Parsons evaded the question. "I've heard—"

"Yes, go on," Louise urged.

"I hesitate to pass on gossip," the elderly woman said. "One hears such wild stories."

"Please tell us everything that you know about the inn," Jean urged. "Louise and I are interested in solving a mystery which started there. That's why we'd like any information you can give us."

"You've seen the ghost at the inn?"

"Only a very live one," Louise answered. "We've heard rumors, though, that there is one. Please tell us what you know about the ghost."

"Stories have been told about one for years, but now I understand that the ghost is becoming active. I've been told that it isn't permitting anyone to enter the building."

"What does it do?" Louise asked.

"According to the rumors I've heard, the mischief-maker snatches clothing from persons who try to get in. One man, I was told, lost a belt with a silver buckle. A woman sightseer had her purse taken."

"How long has this sort of thing been going on?"

"That I can't say. I heard the story only last night at a meeting. Personally, I put little stock in it. In fact, some prankster may have invented the ghost story to have a little fun."

"There may be more to it than that," Louise said

soberly. "Jean and I think someone hides in the building from time to time. He could have started the purse-snatching story to scare people away."

For half an hour longer, the Dana girls chatted with Mrs. Parsons about this possibility but the elderly woman could offer no suggestions as to who the mysterious person might be.

Upon their return to Starhurst School, the sisters went directly to their rooms. As Jean opened the study door she at once noticed a tray of grapes which had been placed on her desk.

"Oh, someone brought us a present while we were away!" she cried in delight. "I love grapes!"

Two large well-formed bunches had been left on a small paper tray. Beside the fruit was a crudely printed note.

Louise picked it up. In astonishment she read:

" 'You must never see your gypsy friends again.' The note is signed '*Dukkerer*.' "

"Dukkerer?" Jean echoed. "Who is he?"

"I don't believe it's a person," Louise reflected as she picked up a book on gypsy words and customs which she had borrowed from the library. "Yes, it's a Romany word. It means fortuneteller. I'll read what it says," Louise went on.

" 'To dukker is to bewitch or to tell a fortune.' Many Romany words have dual meanings. That's because the language is limited in vocabulary."

"A fortuneteller sent these grapes?" Jean asked, puzzled. "It must have been Sebenca!"

"The message isn't encouraging," Louise reflected. "She evidently doesn't want us to find the tribe."

"Or Nura, either."

The girls became thoughtful, reflecting upon the many strange events which had occurred since they had met the beautiful gypsy girl. First she had asked their help, then vanished.

So many questions remained unanswered. Would the mystery ever be solved? For instance, who had knocked out Louise in the woods? Was it the same person who had later snatched the kerchief from her neck?

And how had the scarf happened to turn up at the Franklyn jewelry store? Was it planted by the thief? And if so, had this been done to throw suspicion on Nura?

Equally puzzling was the unexplained attack upon Jean the night of Professor Stanley's first lecture. The Danas had questioned the night watchman and other school employees. None of them had seen an unidentified person on the premises.

And why was Professor Stanley so intent on keeping the Danas away from the inn?

As for the silver spoon, not a clue to it had turned up. Knowing that the dormitory theft had embarrassed Mrs. Crandall, Louise and Jean had not pressed the matter. They felt, however, that if the thief could be caught, it might help to explain other mysteries centering around the abandoned Crossroads Inn.

"Do you suppose," said Louise, "that there is any special significance to this gift of grapes?"

Jean shrugged. "I can't guess. But we may as well enjoy the fruit in any case. Here goes!"

Selecting the smaller of the two bunches, she handed the other to her sister. Jean then popped two plump grapes into her mouth.

"O-oh!" she squealed, making a wry face. "Bitter!"

Louise also had taken a grape, but finding the fruit too sour to eat, she took it out of her mouth instantly.

"I've never tasted such awful grapes!" she exclaimed.

Jean's face remained twisted into a grimace. She sank into a chair, holding her stomach.

"What's wrong?" Louise demanded, rushing to her sister's side.

"I think I've been poisoned!" Jean gasped.

CHAPTER XVII

Suspicion

AT FIRST Louise thought her sister was clowning because the grapes had tasted so sour. But in a moment
she realized that Jean actually was in pain.

Louise became alarmed. A bitter taste lingered in
her own mouth, even though she had swallowed none
of the fruit. Perhaps the grapes *had* been poisoned!

"Quick, Jean!" she cried, pulling the girl to her feet.
"We'd better go to the infirmary!"

Taking a bunch of grapes with them, they hurried
up the stairs to the infirmary. They were fortunate
to find the nurse on duty. Excitedly Louise told the
young woman of her fear that Jean had eaten a
poisoned grape.

"If she reacted so quickly, the poison must be very
powerful!" the nurse cried. "We may have to use a
stomach pump."

"Oh, no!" Jean wailed.

"You may die if we don't get that poison out of you fast," the nurse told her.

"I feel better now," Jean insisted, though her face was beaded with perspiration. "Honestly I do. The pain is passing."

"Lie down while I get things ready," the nurse directed, pointing to a bed in an inner room. To Louise she said in an undertone, "Please phone Dr. Evans. Then go to the chemistry teacher. We may need a fast analysis of those grapes."

As Louise dashed to the telephone in the infirmary office, she heard giggling outside. But when she looked out the door no one was in sight.

"Could that have been Lettie and Ina?" she thought. "They're just heartless enough to laugh at a thing like this."

Louise got in touch with Dr. Evans, then rushed to the study of Miss Brown, the chemistry teacher, taking the grapes with her. Breathlessly she told the story.

"I'll rush a test right through," Miss Brown promised, and hurried off to her laboratory with the grapes. Louise went back to the infirmary. To her relief, Jean was feeling better.

"The nurse says that it won't be necessary to use a stomach pump," she told her sister gleefully.

"Oh, I'm so glad," Louise murmured.

While they were talking, Dr. Evans hurried in. A quick examination followed. He said that he was inclined to agree with the nurse's report but would wait for the chemical analysis before prescribing any medication.

Within ten minutes Miss Brown came to report that vinegar had been poured over some of the grapes in each bunch and soda solution over the rest. Although the combination was harmless, it would produce instant but temporary pain.

"So it was all a joke," Jean said angrily.

"A joke carried to a point of inconveniencing too many people," Dr. Evans commented.

The Danas apologized for being the reason for the physician's unnecessary call and thanked the others for their attention. Back in their room, Louise told her sister of the giggles she had heard in the hallway.

"I'll bet that Lettie and Ina were responsible for the fruit and that note, too!"

"Lettie could have bought the vinegar and she probably took the soda solution from the chem lab. I wish you'd caught them!" said Jean heatedly.

"So do I. But we may yet."

"How?"

"Give me a little time to think it over."

When the gong for supper sounded, Jean insisted upon going to the dining room, declaring that she felt fine. By a system of rotation on which Mrs. Crandall insisted, she and Lettie found themselves, together with four other students, at the headmistress's table.

Jean was seated with Lettie on one side and Professor Stanley on the other. As they sat down, Lettie commented loudly:

"Why, Jean Dana, you look positively ill. What made you so pale?"

Jean ignored the question. She turned her back upon Lettie and began to talk with Professor Stanley. Hoping to find out something from Lettie about the joke, she brought up the subject of gypsy customs. Curious, Lettie leaned over.

"Maybe you've had some new contacts with the gypsies, Jean?" she asked, breaking into the conversation.

"No," Jean replied. "Have you?"

Lettie flushed and kept still. Jean, again directing her attention to Professor Stanley, began discussing gypsy fortunetellers. Deliberately she used the word *dukkerer*, purposely mispronouncing it.

Lettie, eager to show up Jean's supposed ignorance, said quickly, "Oh, Jean, your Romany is priceless! You should say *doochrer*."

"No, Lettie," Professor Stanley corrected her. "I told you the proper pronunciation is *duckrer*."

Suddenly the lecturer darted a glance at Jean, as if he suspected the ruse. Secretly she was delighted that her scheme had worked!

"You speak Romany, Professor Stanley?" she asked in surprise.

The lecturer flushed and there was a glint of anger in his dark eyes as he looked at Lettie. "I've picked up a few words in my study of languages," he answered evenly.

"Then perhaps you can tell me the meaning of the work *kris*."

Professor Stanley looked hard at Jean, as if trying to read her thoughts.

"Sorry," he returned after a long pause. "I can't help you."

During the remainder of the meal, Professor Stanley talked exclusively to Mrs. Crandall. He seemed relieved when dinner was over and then disappeared. Lettie and Ina also vanished, so that Jean had no chance to question them about the tray of grapes.

"I know that they're the ones who played the joke— Lettie gave it away at dinner." She told Louise of the conversation and Professor Stanley's slip of the tongue. "We ought to play a joke of our own on her," Jean added.

"Well, let's return the grapes, anyway."

"We have only one bunch. The other is in the chem lab."

"One will do," Louise decided. "Ina can have that. We'll play a different joke on Lettie. I have an idea!"

She whispered it to her sister. Then, waiting for a time when Lettie and Ina were out of their suite, the Danas slipped in. The untouched bunch of grapes was left on a table by Ina's bed.

Jean and Louise rigged up a dummy from several pillows. They found a bright red skirt draped over one of the chairs, and a brilliant yellow peasant blouse on Ina's bed.

After stuffing the pillow dummy into these, Jean and Louise tied a green scarf about the "head" and propped up the dummy on Lettie's bed.

"You know what's missing?" Jean asked as they gazed critically at their handiwork.

"Beads—jewelry!" Louise exclaimed.

"And here's plenty of that spread all over the top of Lettie's dressing table," Jean cried.

Two necklaces and several pins from Lettie's notoriously gaudy collection completed the effect to the Danas' satisfaction.

In front of the dummy, Louise placed a sign with the word *dukkerer* on it.

"We must leave a note!" Jean chuckled. "What shall we say?"

"Let me," Louise asked, reaching for a pad and pencil. "I've picked up a few Romany words from that book and can put them to use now." After a moment's thought, she grinned and printed:

Beware interfering with Romany buci.

"That word *buci* should worry Lettie and Ina!" Jean chuckled. "What does it mean?"

"'Romany business,'" Louise translated. "Lettie will have to dash straight to Professor Stanley to find out what it means."

The girls placed the note in the hand of the dummy fortuneteller. Tiptoeing unseen from the suite, they took turns with Doris and Evelyn watching from an alcove for the return of Lettie and Ina.

Nearly half an hour elapsed, with Evelyn on duty, before the two arrived. Both were in an unpleasant mood, arguing over an algebra assignment.

"You expect me to do most of your homework for you," Ina complained.

"You should help me out when I'm so busy," Lettie retorted.

She opened the door to their bedroom, stopping short as she saw the tray of grapes beside Ina's bed.

"Ina! Did you bring those wretched things back here?"

"I certainly did not!"

"Then the Dana girls must have guessed our joke!" she cried. "And look what they've propped up in my bed."

The door closed and Evelyn could hear no more. But she waved a handkerchief to the other girls as a signal to be ready for action. Within a minute Lettie came bolting out of the room, Louise's note clutched in her hand.

"She can't figure out that word *buci*," Jean chuckled. "We must follow her! This will be good."

Lettie went directly to Professor Stanley's room. Louise, Jean, Evelyn, and Doris followed but took a route through the large lounge into a small adjoining parlor. It opened into the hall directly opposite the first-floor guest room. Unaware that the four girls were listening, Lettie pounded on the door of the lecturer's room. Finally he opened it.

"What is it, Lettie?" he asked wearily. "Haven't I asked you not to come here to talk with me? Do you want Mrs. Crandall to become suspicious?"

"This is important or I wouldn't have bothered you. See! The Dana girls left a note in my room. One word is in Romany. I don't know its meaning."

"Let me see that note." Professor Stanley took it from Lettie.

"Do you know the word?" she asked eagerly.

"Of course. It means 'gypsy business.'"

"'Beware interfering in gypsy business,'" Lettie read slowly. "What do the Danas mean by that? Maybe they know—"

"Don't speculate," the lecturer interrupted. "Watch Louise and Jean and report to me where they go and what they do."

"I'll be glad to! They think they're the only ones who can solve a mystery. We'll show them, won't we, Professor Stanley?"

"Remember your instructions," the man returned coldly. "Now get back to your room before you're seen here."

"Yes, sir," Lettie answered, backing off. "You can

depend on me to watch Jean and Louise. I'll never let them out of my sight."

She hurried up the stairs. The other girls had a hearty laugh, knowing how easy it would be to outwit Lettie. Louise, though, was disturbed by her reference to Professor Stanley working on the mystery.

"Ina hinted that someone besides Lettie might be in on it," she reminded her sister. "Maybe she meant Professor Stanley."

"If he's involved in the gypsy business," Louise said thoughtfully, "I certainly think that Mrs. Crandall should know about it."

"I agree," said Jean, and their friends nodded. "First thing tomorrow morning I'll tell her."

CHAPTER XVIII

A Sudden Disappearance

BEFORE breakfast the next morning, Jean and Louise were at the door of Mrs. Crandall's office.

"Good morning, girls," the headmistress greeted them cordially. "Come in."

"May we speak privately with you for a moment?" Louise requested.

"Why, of course."

Surprised by the request, Mrs. Crandall took the girls into an inner office where their conversation would not be overheard by a student secretary. Jean closed the door.

"What is it, Louise?" the headmistress asked, after the three had seated themselves. "Have you found the silver spoon?"

"No, Mrs. Crandall. We came to talk to you about Professor Stanley. You don't mind if Jean and I ask a few direct questions?"

"On the contrary, I wish you would come straight to the point," the headmistress urged. "You have some criticism of Professor Stanley that you think I should know?"

"We distrust him, Mrs. Crandall," Louise replied. "Our suspicions may not be too well founded, but we thought that we ought to tell you what they are."

"I'm glad you came to me. Feel free to say whatever you wish."

"First, are you satisfied that Professor Stanley is a bona fide lecturer?"

Mrs. Crandall looked surprised at the question and hesitated several seconds before she replied, "I must confess that in many ways Professor Stanley has been disappointing. As for his lectures, I accepted him wholly upon the recommendation of a lecture bureau."

"Isn't it unusual that he has stayed so long?" Jean commented. "Apparently he hasn't many engagements to fill."

The headmistress nodded. "Now that I recall, the letter from the lecture bureau came only a short time before Professor Stanley arrived."

"The bureau hasn't contacted you since you received the letter?" Louise asked.

"No, I would have sent a check in payment for Professor Stanley's talks, but he asked me for the amount in cash. I paid him last night."

Worried by the Dana girls' inquiries, Mrs. Crandall urged them to tell her everything that they suspected about the lecturer. They were tempted to mention his close association with Lettie in solving some mystery but refrained from doing so.

"Professor Stanley is thoroughly familiar with the Romany language," Louise answered. "And for several reasons Jean and I have even wondered if he may have some connection with the gypsies."

"Oh, dear me!" Mrs. Crandall gasped, taken aback. "Such a possibility never occurred to me. I assure you I'll look into his background at once!"

The headmistress admitted then that the man's behavior at Starhurst School had begun to annoy her.

"He has filled the heads of several girls with silly ideas about dreams," she commented. "Then, too, he failed to deliver several lectures which had been scheduled, without offering any explanation. As for the lectures he did present—well, they have not been up to the standard I've maintained in the past."

Mrs. Crandall thanked Louise and Jean for coming to her with the information. She promised that she would check with the lecture bureau and also talk to Professor Stanley about his credentials.

Satisfied that they had done all they could, the girls went on to breakfast. At the head table, Jean found herself between two empty chairs. Lettie Briggs, as usual, had overslept. Professor Stanley was also absent.

This struck Jean as odd, for the lecturer had a hearty appetite.

When breakfast was over, Mrs. Crandall said she was going directly to the professor's room. She invited the girls to follow at a discreet distance. Repeatedly, the headmistress rapped on the door. There was no response.

Convinced that the man was not in the room, Mrs. Crandall opened the door. The bed was rumpled and newspapers were scattered about untidily. The headmistress opened the wardrobe closet and peered inside. Professor Stanley's suitcase and all his clothing had been removed!

"Why, he's gone!" the headmistress exclaimed. "And without notifying me or thanking me for my hospitality!"

The sisters' suspicions mounted by the moment.

"I'll telephone the Silverton Lecture Bureau at once," Mrs. Crandall told the girls. "Will you check the room to see if he left anything? Apparently your ideas were sound!"

Louise and Jean gathered up the newspapers and examined bureau drawers. The room seemed to be bare of clues.

"Professor Stanley was careful not to leave any evidence behind," Jean said grimly. "I think my questions yesterday may have upset him!"

"Evidently," Louise answered, poking in the scrap

basket. "The police may be closing in on Stanley."

"You think he may be a thief, then?"

"He's hiding something. I'm curious to learn what report the lecture bureau will make on him."

"Lettie may be able to throw a little light on his sudden leave-taking," Jean remarked. "We ought to give her the third degree."

Louise emptied the contents of the wastepaper basket on the rug. At the bottom of the metal container, amid cigarette ashes, she came upon several scraps of torn gray paper.

"Find anything?" Jean asked.

"I'm not sure. These torn bits have writing on them. The words are in Romany, too," Louise added excitedly.

"Maybe we can fit them together!" Jean proposed.

Piece by piece, the sisters put the torn paper together. Familiar words such as cirikle and tsera began to fall into place.

"Do you realize what this is?" Jean suddenly demanded, rocking back on her heels. "It's a copy of the message that was printed on the green kerchief!"

"You're right, Jean!"

The girls were exclaiming over their important discovery when Mrs. Crandall appeared in the doorway.

"The situation is very serious," the headmistress reported. "I telephoned the lecture bureau, and learned that they have no Professor Stanley on their lists."

"He's a phony then?" Jean cried.

"I'm afraid so," Mrs. Crandall acknowledged.

"He must have forged the original letter from the lecture bureau," Louise guessed, "and showed up here before you had a chance to confirm the engagement."

"And that explains why he insisted I pay him in cash instead of through the lecture bureau," Mrs. Crandall added. "But who is the man? Why did he come here? And where is he now?"

"You'll notify the police?" Louise suggested.

"This very moment! Have you girls found any clues which might help the authorities trace him."

Jean displayed the pieced-together paper with the Romany writing on it.

"Glue it together, and I'll see that it is taken to police headquarters," the headmistress urged. "Professor Stanley must be apprehended. He has taken money under false pretenses."

Louise mentioned that Lettie Briggs possibly might have an inkling of where the man had gone. She had talked with him a great deal.

"With your permission, Jean and I will question her," Louise volunteered.

"Please do, girls."

Louise glanced at her wrist watch. "It's nine-twenty now. I have a lab period in ten minutes."

"And I have a history class," said Jean.

"Never mind that," the headmistress said. "I'll excuse both of you and Lettie as well. Just find her and talk to her. Learn what you can and report everything to me."

After a search, the Dana girls found Lettie walking through the downstairs lounge.

"Will you please come with us for a little walk?" Louise invited her. "Jean and I want to talk to you."

"About what?" Lettie demanded suspiciously.

"Professor Stanley."

Lettie tossed her head. "I don't care to discuss him with you. Anyway, I have a class."

"Mrs. Crandall has excused all of us because this is very important," Jean said.

"You're kidding."

"We're not, Lettie. Did you know that Professor Stanley left here very mysteriously?"

"Left the school?" Lettie could not hide her astonishment. "Are—are you sure?"

"His room is empty. We want to talk to you about it." Jean took Lettie's arm, steering her out of the dormitory.

Obviously shaken by the news that the lecturer had left the institution, Lettie permitted the Danas to guide her into the garden.

"It can't be true that Professor Stanley has gone!" she insisted. "He promised to see me today."

"Lettie, he accepted money from Mrs. Crandall under false pretenses. She has notified the police."

"Oh, no! Why, Professor Stanley was so brilliant." Lettie was almost in tears.

"Dishonest might be a better word," Louise corrected her. "What did he tell you about himself, Lettie? That he was a gypsy?"

"Of course not! He couldn't have been."

Questioned relentlessly by the Danas, Lettie finally admitted that she knew very little about the lecturer, despite her bragging.

"He did say he expects to teach at Roland Junior College," she recalled. "But that's all I know. Honestly."

The Danas let her go, and Louise and Jean reported their conversation to Mrs. Crandall. The headmistress immediately put through a telephone call to Roland Junior College. She learned that it was true Professor Stanley had joined the teaching staff there.

"But he's not expected until fall, Mrs. Crandall," the dean told her.

Throughout the day, Mrs. Crandall kept in close touch with the police. Railroad and bus stations were checked, as were all taxicab companies. Professor Stanley, it seemed, had dropped completely out of sight.

Though concerned over the situation, the Danas could take no active part in the search because of classes and other school activities, including tennis. Late that afternoon, after several fast sets, they showered and started to leave the gymnasium.

Oddly enough, many of the students in the dressing room did not speak of their game. This was unusual, for both girls had played exceedingly well.

"It looks as if we're being ignored," Jean remarked on their way to their rooms. "I can't figure it out."

"It did strike me that the girls were looking at us in a peculiar way," Louise returned. "I can't imagine what's wrong."

To the astonishment of the sisters, their schoolmates appeared no more friendly the following day. Wherever Louise and Jean went, they encountered curious stares.

Not until late that afternoon did they gain a hint of what might be wrong. They were busy with homework when Doris Harland burst into their study. Greatly agitated, she waved a torn letter before their startled eyes.

"Louise! Jean!" she cried. "Tell me the truth! You're not gypsies, are you?"

CHAPTER XIX

A Disturbing Note

"JEAN and I gypsies?" Louise asked, bursting into laughter at Doris's question.

"Whatever gave you such a ridiculous idea?" Jean exclaimed. "Do you think we look like gypsies?"

"Louise could pass for one," Doris answered honestly. "She's dark. But that's not all. The girls are saying that you two aren't really sisters."

"Why?" Louise demanded, the smile fading from her face. "Doris, you aren't serious!"

"I'm afraid I am, Louise. Haven't you and Jean noticed how some of the girls have been acting toward you?"

"Yes, we have," Louise admitted, "but what's behind it? Lettie?"

"Not this time. It's a note in a man's handwriting."

She delved into her pocket and brought out a crumpled note. Louise and Jean quickly read the bold scrawl.

The Danas are not really sisters. They were adopted from a gypsy tribe. Louise looks like one, and Jean probably takes after her gajo father.

The two girls stared at each other stupefied. Finally Louise spoke.

"This is wicked and malicious. Doris, where did you get this note?"

"From Alice Heady. The note has been handed to everyone in school, I'm afraid."

"It's some sort of trick!" Jean asserted angrily. "But why would—"

"Then none of it is true?" Doris interrupted. "It wouldn't make any difference to me—"

"Of course it isn't true," Louise said quickly. "After our parents died, Jean and I were adopted by Uncle Ned and Aunt Harriet Dana—our father's brother and sister. Our mother was blonde, like Jean, and I have my father's dark hair and complexion. That's why we don't look too much alike."

"I wonder who would make up a vicious story like this," Jean said, frowning at the note. "If Professor Stanley were here, I'd suspect him."

"He may have mailed the note to Lettie," Doris commented.

"Let's ask Mrs. Crandall if she has a sample of his handwriting," Louise proposed. "I'd like to compare it with this!"

The headmistress was shocked when she read the note and declared that the writer should be severely chastised. But she could not furnish a sample of Professor Stanley's handwriting. In leaving Starhurst School, the lecturer had taken with him every paper which might have provided a clue.

"I'll question all the students," Mrs. Crandall decided.

The note was traced to a sophomore named Edna Gorman. The girl readily explained that she had found it on a garden path.

"I showed it to some of my friends," she admitted. "I didn't realize that it would cause such a stir. I'm sorry."

"Don't worry about it," Louise told her kindly when she heard about it. "Not too much harm has been done. Just tell all your friends that the note is untrue. Jean and I are sisters, and we have no gypsy blood."

Not only Edna, but Doris and Evelyn as well, did everything they could to put an end to the false rumor. Evelyn was convinced that Lettie had planted the damaging note in the garden. But who, she said to Doris, had penned it for her?

"I can't believe that she's been in touch with Professor Stanley since he left here," Evelyn mused. "Maybe he wrote it for her before he skipped out."

No one could explain how the note had chanced to be lying on the garden path. The gardener and the night watchman had seen no stranger on the premises.

Lettie herself maintained an aloof attitude toward

the entire matter, haughtily refusing to answer any questions. Evelyn and Doris became more convinced than ever that she knew a great deal more than she would tell.

Meanwhile, Louise and Jean were far more concerned over Professor Stanley's disappearance than the wild story about themselves. From Mrs. Crandall they learned that the police had made no progress in tracing him. Chief Riley was of the opinion that the name Stanley was an alias and that the missing man might have a police record under another name.

"Maybe Professor Stanley is a banished gypsy!" Jean told Louise as they left the office and headed for their mailbox.

"From Nura's tribe!" her sister exclaimed.

The more she thought about it, the more she thought it might be true. That might account for his wanting to stay at the school. During his absences on various kinds of errands he could have committed thievery. And no one would have thought of looking for him at Starhurst!

"It all sounds logical," said Jean when she heard her sister's conclusions. "Well, hurray, here's some mail for us."

Stuffed in the box was a small package from Aunt Harriet, and a letter in an unfamiliar hand addressed to them both. The envelope was cheap and soiled.

Curious, Jean ripped it open. Her face brightened. "It's from Sebenca!" she announced.

The note merely requested the Danas to meet her at four o'clock the following afternoon at the Crossroads Inn.

"We don't know Sebenca's handwriting," Louise said. "This may be a trick."

"On the other hand, do we dare pass up a chance to talk to her again? She may know what became of Professor Stanley."

"At least Sebenca can tell us where the gypsy camp moved," Louise nodded. "That information would be valuable to the police."

Louise showed the note to Mrs. Crandall and asked permission to go. At first the headmistress was hesitant to permit the Danas to meet the gypsy fortuneteller, but finally she said:

"All right, if you'll take a policeman with you."

"Gypsies distrust all police," Louise pointed out. "I'm sure that Sebenca would run away the moment she glimpsed a uniform."

"I suppose you are right," Mrs. Crandall admitted. "Very well, you may go. But I insist that both Miss Parker and my husband accompany you to the crossroads."

On the way back to their rooms, Louise and Jean opened their package from Aunt Harriet. "Two pairs of hand-knit tennis socks! Isn't she the old darling!" Jean exclaimed.

At three-thirty the next day the four drove off.

Not far from the inn they found Sebenca awaiting them. Louise and Jean gave sighs of relief and introduced their companions.

"What news have you of Nura?" the old fortune-teller eagerly asked the Danas.

When they told her that they had none, a look of dismay spread over her face. Neither she nor Jiva had heard a word from the gypsy girl.

"I'm dreadfully sorry," said Louise.

Then she asked Sebenca if the woman were acquainted with a Professor Stanley. She shook her head.

"We suspect that he is a gypsy using a false name," Louise said, then described the lecturer.

"Ah!" Sebenca's face became animated. "This man is well-educated?"

"Yes, indeed," Jean assured her. "He speaks several languages, including Romany."

"All gypsies know many languages," Sebenca answered. "This professor—he has small, very piercing eyes?"

"Yes."

"I know a gypsy such as you describe. His name is not Stanley. It is Mixail Nikola."

"A member of your tribe?"

Sebenca made a gesture of derision. "No, and he would never be welcome at our fire. Nikola is always in trouble with the police. That is because he is a thief. Nikola is bad."

"Where would he be likely to go?" Louise asked.

The fortuneteller's answer was an expressive shrug. "Who knows? Nikola speaks Romany. If he asked food at any gypsy camp where he was not known, it would be given to him."

Sebenca's information elated the Danas. If Professor Stanley were Nikola and he was hiding in a gypsy camp, the police should find him easily!

Changing the subject, Jean asked, "Sebenca, why did King Sando break camp near Franklyn? And where is your tribe now?"

Sebenca gestured toward the old inn. "Follow the trail for a quarter of a mile along the brook," she directed. "Then turn left at the forked maple. Keep walking and you will see the camp if your eyes are sharp."

So the gypsies were not hiding!

"Why did King Sando leave the Franklyn area in such a hurry?" Jean went on.

"Our water supply gave out," the woman replied.

"Well, I'm glad to learn the reason," said Jean. "Did you know that you're under suspicion?"

"Why?"

When Jean told her of the jewelry-store robbery, Sebenca raised herself to her full height, putting her chin high in the air.

"My people do not rob jewelry stores!" she said haughtily.

King Sando may have trouble convincing the police of that," Louise warned the fortuneteller. "We're worried for Nura, too."

She then told Sebenca about the green kerchief which had been picked up in the Franklyn jewelry store. The gypsy woman became excited.

"My people are innocent!" she cried, twisting her hands. "They would not steal!"

"Zarka?" Jean prompted.

Sebenca hesitated, then shook her head. "Zarka is mean and tricky," she said. "He will cheat in a game of cards or a horse deal. But Zarka would not rob a gajo, for fear of bringing King Sando's anger upon his head."

"Where is Zarka now?" questioned Louise.

Sebenca replied that she had not seen him in many days. "Sometimes he takes a meal in the camp. Then he will be gone for a while. Zarka is a law unto himself."

The gypsy woman had grown restless. Evidently disturbed by the news which Jean and Louise had given her, she quickly bade them good-by.

"*Dza devles!* God go with you!" she murmured, quietly slipping away.

After Sebenca had left, the girls wondered if they had been wise in revealing so much to her. She would give a warning to her people and they might really go into hiding.

"I rate the number one dunce cap," Jean berated herself.

Miss Parker felt sorry for the young sleuth. To cheer her up, she said kindly, "While we're here let's investigate the inn. I never have seen the inside of it. I'm sure that with four of us together it will be safe. Don't you think so, Professor Crandall?"

"What possible harm in it?" He smiled.

The Danas were delighted. But chills of excitement raced up and down their spines. Would they meet the thieving ghost?

With Louise holding a flashlight, the four set off for the inn. As before, entry was obtained through the front window.

Once inside the dark building, they moved cautiously. The search was not very rewarding. No one was found lurking in the rooms, nor were there any new clues to the various angles of the mystery.

Gradually relaxing and becoming less alert to danger, they meandered along a first-floor hall toward the old carriage entrance. Jean, Miss Parker, and Professor Crandall lagged some distance behind Louise, who carried the light.

One moment the girl's flashlight beam was visible. The next instant it had vanished.

A terrified scream from the darkness told the others what must have happened. Louise had plunged through the decayed flooring into the cellar!

CHAPTER XX

Louise Pleads a Case

"Louise!" Jean cried frantically. "Where are you?"

There was no response in the dark, ramshackle building as Jean stumbled forward, groping her way along the wall.

"Careful!" warned Professor Crandall. He lighted a match and they both saw Miss Parker ahead of them. "This flooring is very treacherous. Without a light—"

His words were interrupted by another scream. This time the cry had come from Miss Parker, who also had crashed through.

"Help me! Help!" she called. "O-oh!"

Jean and Professor Crandall heard a loud thud, then a moan. By the light of another match they hurried forward and paused at the edge of a gaping square opening in the floor.

As Jean peered down, she saw Miss Parker pain-

159

fully pulling herself to a sitting position on a flight of stone steps.

"Are you badly hurt?" Jean called anxiously.

"I'm all right. Just shaken," Miss Parker murmured. "No! No! Don't try to come down. It's too dangerous."

At that moment they were all electrified by a flashlight turned on them from below and a voice saying, "Hello, everybody!"

"Louise! Is that you?" Jean cried unbelievingly.

"No one else," came the cheerful, muffled reply from the bottom of the steps. "I tumbled all the way down."

"Thank goodness, you're both all right," Professor Crandall murmured in relief.

"I'm coming down!" Jean announced.

"Don't. You'll ruin your clothes," Louise advised. "This place is covered with cobwebs."

"What's down there?"

"Only a small storage room," Louise reported, "and the floor is solid. I'll see what else there is."

As Jean and Professor Crandall helped Miss Parker, they noted that actually she had not fallen through a decayed section of the flooring. A trap door had been lifted up against the wall and left open.

"The cellar must have been used in Civil War days as a hiding place for slaves who were escaping to freedom!" Professor Crandall announced, inspecting the big brass hinges on the trap door. "The wood is solid oak."

Below, Louise was busy exploring.

"What's the place like?" Jean called down eagerly.

"It's cut up into small rooms," Louise reported. "All empty."

"No wells?"

"None that I can find. No hidden loot, either. I'll look around a bit more—"

"No, Louise," Miss Parker firmly put an end to this plan. "Some other day, perhaps. We must return to Starhurst." The fall had dampened the teacher's enthusiasm for further exploration.

Reluctantly Louise came up from the basement. She had not injured herself, but her hair and clothes were a mass of cobwebs. Treading carefully, she followed the others.

Scarcely had the four sightseers crawled out into the sunlight than they saw a group of people coming through the woods.

"State policemen!" Miss Parker exclaimed. "At least two of them are. They have someone in custody!"

"A gypsy," Jean said. "Why, he looks like King Sando!"

Behind the policemen trailed the entire gypsy tribe. Angry men, women, and children in bright-colored garb were shouting and shaking their fists in protest.

Fearful that the gypsies would get out of control, the two policemen were hustling their captive along the path.

"Quiet down, you!" one of the policemen shouted, drawing his club.

Several of the gypsies picked up stones.

"If something isn't done quickly, there will be a dreadful fight!" Louise exclaimed.

Impulsively she started forward to meet the two officers. Jean kept close behind, with Professor Crandall and Miss Parker bringing up the rear.

"What seems to be the trouble?" Louise asked the policemen.

Her question probably would have been ignored if one of the officers had not recognized the Dana girls.

"You're the sisters Chief Riley was telling me about only a few days ago, aren't you?"

"Yes, we are."

"Then I'll tell you. We're arresting this gypsy on suspicion."

"In connection with the Franklyn jewelry-store theft?" Louise asked.

"That's right. The chief ordered us to find the gypsies that had skipped out and bring in their leader."

"Do you have evidence against him?"

"Our job is to make the arrest," the officer replied. "The rest is up to Captain Smith."

Louise and Jean knew that it would be useless to

try to dissuade the men from carrying out their orders. Accordingly, they merely asked permission to follow the police car to headquarters.

"All right," the policeman agreed. "We must move fast, though, or the mob will try to snatch Sando."

Louise found Sebenca in the crowd and urged the fortuneteller to keep her people from making trouble.

"Tell them that Sando will be fairly treated," Jean said persuasively. "If he's innocent, he'll come right back."

Sebenca repeated this advice in Romany. Her words seemed to carry weight, because the gypsies dropped their stones. Though they continued to taunt the policemen, they made no aggressive moves.

The Danas, Miss Parker, and Professor Crandall followed the police car to headquarters. Behind them trailed a half-dozen automobiles loaded with gypsies. Louise and Jean noted that Zarka was not in the throng.

At the police station there was great confusion. Gypsies swarmed over the place, demanding King Sando's release. Captain Smith gave orders to rush the case through.

King Sando was charged with larceny. In a torrent of mixed English and Romany, he denied all knowledge of the jewelry-store theft. Then he asked why the police thought he was guilty.

"We found this in the store," the captain told him.

He held up the green kerchief. King Sando looked stunned. Apparently he recognized the scarf as belonging to his daughter. He did not speak.

At this point, Louise rose and asked if she might speak in the defendant's behalf. The police captain looked amazed but granted the permission.

Louise made a straightforward statement about how she and her sister had found the kerchief and how it had been snatched away. She explained that at the time the tribe was many miles distant from Penfield.

"I think it's very likely that the person who took the scarf was the one that robbed the store," she said.

Louise then told him that a duplicate of the Romany message had turned up in Professor Stanley's room at Starhurst School.

"We have reason to believe that he is an impostor," she said.

"Clearly this is not a simple case of larceny," the captain remarked as Louise sat down. After thanking her, he said, "All police have been alerted to look for this Professor Stanley. And in view of Miss Dana's testimony, I can't order King Sando held in jail."

The gypsies gave a shout of glee. "Sando, will you agree to remain within call of the court? We may need you as a witness later on."

"I give a gypsy's word," the king replied proudly.

He smiled a little. "A gypsy may lie to the police in English," he said. "But not in Romany. I will give you my promise in Romany."

Captain Smith smiled back. "Very well, we will accept your promise in the Romany language," he agreed.

King Sando solemnly gave it, and the case was dismissed. Immediately the gypsies swarmed about Louise to thank her. Two of the women affectionately kissed her on the cheek.

The gypsy leader solemnly shook the girl's hand. "You are a friend," he said. "Sando will never forget. If we were unkind to you, we are sorry."

Louise felt that the moment was right to press the gypsy king for forgiveness of his daughter Nura.

"Nura loves Stivo," she declared. "It would be most unfair to make her wed Zarka."

King Sando scowled at mention of the insolent young gypsy. "I no longer trust Zarka," he muttered. "He would make himself king!"

"Then why not forgive Nura for running away? Let her marry Stivo and be happy."

The gypsy leader's reply delighted the girls. "I will forgive my daughter on one condition," he said. "It must be proven that Stivo did not steal the skafidi from our people."

"We'll do it!" Jean declared.

The leader of the gypsies seemed eager for news of

his daughter. He told Louise and Jean that his wife, Jiva, had grieved for her to the point of illness.

"Will you help me find Nura?" he pleaded. "Tell her she will not be punished if she returns to our tent."

"We'll deliver the message if we can find her," Louise promised. "Our only clue is the writing on the kerchief." She turned to Captain Smith. "May I have it, please?"

The officer handed it to Louise and she gave it to Sando.

Holding it in his hands, he stared at the piece of silk.

"What do the words mean?" Louise asked eagerly.

Tears glistened in King Sando's eyes. Deeply moved by the message, he was unable to speak.

CHAPTER XXI

A New Lead

RECOVERING his composure, King Sando translated the Romany writing for the Dana girls.

" 'Like a wounded bird, I fly from the danger here. I will hide in the tent of Varia for three days. We will marry before their tribunal.' "

"Stivo never got this message," Louise explained to Nura's father.

"And more than three days have passed since she wrote it," added Jean. "Poor Nura! She probably thinks that Stivo has changed his mind."

"Who is Varia?" Louise asked thoughtfully.

"A fortuneteller in Chicago," King Sando revealed. "She is with a tribe outside that city."

"Stivo should go there at once on a chance that Nura is still with Varia," Louise declared. "With your permission, King Sando, Jean and I will try to get word to him."

"Do so," the gypsy leader agreed. "I may have made a mistake in opposing the marriage. Find Nura and Stivo and I promise you they will have a hearing."

Louise at once called the Rose Tree Restaurant where Stivo was employed. The young violinist was not in, but Jean left a message for him to call her at Starhurst School. Late that evening he called. Greatly excited by Nura's message, he told Louise that he would take the first plane to Chicago.

"I can't understand why Nura ran away from the inn," he said. "What is this danger she fears?"

Louise said that she did not know. Privately, she and Jean wondered if the gypsy girl might not have been frightened away from the inn permanently by the phony policeman.

Was it possible that Mixail Nikola, alias Professor Stanley, was the fake policeman and also the thieving ghost? The Danas began to wonder if Nikola, rather than Zarka, might have stolen the tribal skafidi and the missing jewelry.

"Oh, where is that man?" Jean fumed when morning came and the police still had not found him.

The girls were told that there had been a big theft of old silver and jewelry from a Penfield home. The man had been seen, but got away. They wondered if the new theft tied in with their mystery.

The day was a trying one for Louise and Jean. Classwork seemed particularly difficult and both girls found it hard to concentrate. Their thoughts were centered on Nura. Would Stivo find her?

In the middle of the afternoon the girls received a telephone call from him. Completely dejected, he reported failure.

"Nura had left by the time I reached Chicago," he said. "She stayed with Varia until yesterday morning, then went away believing that I no longer wanted to marry her. No one knows where she went."

"Oh, what a shame!" Louise exclaimed. "But don't give up hope, Stivo."

"Oh, it's no use," the musician insisted dolefully.

To comfort the brokenhearted gypsy, Louise suggested that Nura might return to Franklyn with the idea of rejoining her people.

"But the gypsy camp has moved!" Stivo cried despairingly.

"Someone can be stationed at the old camp site to watch for her," Louise proposed. "Suppose I try to arrange that."

"Yes, yes," Stivo said quickly.

"I'll let you know the instant we have any word," Louise promised.

After relaying the conversation to Jean, the Danas decided that it might be best not to tell King Sando of the plan, since Nura might become suspicious of any guard sent by her father. The person to help them was Sebenca.

"She'll keep it a secret and send a trustworthy watcher," Jean said.

"We must see Sebenca at once before Nura runs away from Franklyn," Louise urged. "Let's ask Miss Parker to go with us."

The two girls found the teacher correcting quiz papers. Regretfully she told them that she could not take time from the work.

Next, the Danas tried Professor Crandall. He was in his study, surrounded by a stack of books and a mass of untidy papers.

"It's four o'clock now," he said. "Much too late for me to go. I have to give a talk this evening." As the girls started to leave, he added, "I've been reading about gypsies. A fascinating people! The majority arrived in this country during the last quarter of the nineteenth century. More than half of them use Romany as their native tongue."

"Yes," said the Danas politely, edging for the door.

"The gypsies, I've learned, have their own courts which are called *romano kris*, conducted in the manner of the gypsylike people of India. Punishments may be expulsion from the tribe—*mahrime*—or fines."

"Yes, Professor Crandall."

"Gypsies distrust our courts," he continued. "They prefer to settle their differences among themselves. The tribes have their own complete but primitive government organization. First it is divided according to the country of the gypsies' origin, then subdivided again and again. The smallest unit, the tribe, is presided over by a king."

"That's most interesting," said Louise from the doorway.

"It is said that most gypsy men are lazy." Professor Crandall laughed. "By our standards, I suppose they are. The old-type gypsy lived by horse trading and on his wife's earnings as a fortuneteller. This commercial value of the wife may have led to the practice of requiring payment for a bride."

"It's because of a gyspy bride that we must see Sebenca at once," Louise broke in, speaking rapidly. "Nura has left Chicago and we think that she may return to the old camp at Franklyn. We must find her to let her know about her father's change of heart. We want Sebenca to post lookouts at the deserted camp, so Nura won't leave there before we can talk with her. The poor girl thinks her sweetheart has deserted her and there's no telling where she'll go if she finds her people have left the camp!"

When Louise paused for breath, Jean said quickly:

"It won't take long, Professor Crandall. Please change your mind."

"You girls are very convincing," the professor said, chuckling, "and I'd like nothing better than to go. Unfortunately, I must be at the Penfield Chamber of Commerce dinner by six o'clock. These books on gypsy life so engrossed me that I've neglected to plan my talk. I must do it at once. I'm really sorry."

"We'll have to try to find someone else to go with us," Jean said as the girls sped up the hall.

They began to make the rounds of classroom offices, trying one teacher after another without success.

"What are we going to do?" Jean asked in discouragement. "Go alone, Louise?"

"Not without permission."

"Let's ask Mrs. Crandall. She may let us, under the circumstances."

The headmistress, however, was firm in her opinion that it would not be safe for the girls to visit the area of the Crossroads Inn unescorted.

"I'm quite willing for you to take the station wagon," she consented. "My only requirement is that you have one of the staff with you."

Disconsolately, the sisters left the office.

"We must find someone!" Jean cried desperately. "If we don't see Sebenca today, we may lose our chance to get in touch with Nura!"

CHAPTER XXII

A Telltale Photograph

As the Danas were about ready to ask the night watchman or the gardener to accompany them to the gypsy camp, Professor Crandall came down the hall.

"Oh, here you are!" he said, smiling. "I thought you might have started for the crossroads."

"It doesn't look as if we're going," Louise replied gloomily. "We haven't found anyone to take us."

"I will."

The Danas stared at the professor, wondering if he had forgotten about his dinner engagement and speech.

"When I told you I couldn't go, I completely forgot that I canceled that Chamber of Commerce speech a week ago," he confessed in embarrassment. "Quite a joke on me! In checking my engagement pad, I discovered that I'm free for the next few hours."

"Wonderful!" Jean exclaimed. "Let's start right now."

Within ten minutes the three were en route to the crossroads. The professor parked the station wagon in a clearing, then the trio set off at a brisk pace on the path through the woods. Sebenca's directions for reaching the camp had been accurate. Soon they found it, nestled in a grove of tall beeches.

Immediately Louise and Jean were recognized by the gypsies, who now regarded them as friends. A swarm of laughing, shouting children escorted them to Sebenca's van.

The old fortuneteller arose from a loom on which she was weaving a rug, and smiled a welcome. The girls at once told her the purpose of their visit.

"We will find Nura!" Sebenca said excitedly.

She promised to keep the matter a secret and assign two trustworthy young men to take turns watching for Nura at the deserted camp site near Franklyn.

"It is best that no one else knows what we are doing," the old woman said. "Enemies are everywhere."

"What do you mean?" Louise asked.

"Twice food has been stolen from this camp. King Sando is very angry. He vows vengeance, if the thief can be caught."

She asked her callers to wait a minute while she sent off the first gypsy youth who was to watch for

Nura. When Sebenca came back, Professor Crandall started to question her about tribal customs and background. She answered politely but finally suggested, with a twinkle in her shrewd eyes, that he ought to have his future told.

"Oh, I have no confidence in such things," he protested.

"It will cost you nothing," Sebenca urged.

"Do have your fortune told, Professor Crandall!" Jean pleaded, seizing his hand.

"If Mrs. Crandall should hear of this, I'd never live it down!" he said, but finally he gave in.

From a pocket of her ample skirt, Sebenca took out a deck of cards. Her lips parted as she murmured to herself and motioned for the professor to seat himself at a small table. Dealing out five cards, she gazed intently into his eyes.

"You are to have a long and useful life," she intoned, rapidly dealing more cards. "I see a fine career ahead for you."

Professor Crandall winked at Louise. His future, he thought, was following the routine pattern.

"You have suffered a great loss," Sebenca said suddenly. "Something you treasure far above money."

"Why, I have!" Professor Crandall exclaimed, startled.

"You will find this missing property below many stones."

"My notes, you mean?" Professor Crandall cried in amazement.

Sebenca shrugged and gathered up the cards. She would say no more.

"Now do you believe in fortunetelling, Professor Crandall?" Jean asked, laughing.

"I will when I find my notes! You know, I wonder —do you suppose I could have put those papers in a basement cabinet at Starhurst School?"

"We'll look as soon as we get back," Louise suggested. "Sebenca has given us a new thought."

"Can you tell me anything more definite?" the professor urged the fortuneteller.

The old gypsy woman smiled. Outside, someone had struck up a merry tune on a violin.

"The ceremonial dance begins," Sebenca said. "I must go. You will stay to watch it?"

"We'd love to," Louise accepted the invitation.

Outside, the gypsies had gathered about several musicians. Besides the violinist, there was one playing a cembalo, another a bass viol, and the fourth shook a tambourine.

In the center of the group, a young gypsy girl, keeping time with castanets, was dancing to the fast tempo. Clicking her heels, she lifted her arms in snakelike motions which reminded the watchers of slowly rising smoke.

As Louise and Jean stood apart from Professor

Crandall at the edge of the group of spectators, a youth sidled up to them. He was Zarka! The gypsy was smiling, but he spoke in a terse, ugly tone:

"You keep my Nura in hiding!" Without giving the girls a chance to deny the charge, he went on, "I grant you one day to bring her here! One day!"

The Danas protested that they did not know the missing girl's whereabouts. Zarka ignored their remarks. With another sneering smile, he sauntered away.

Sebenca, who had been watching the little scene, quickly joined the girls. Anxiously she asked them what Zarka had said. Jean repeated his threat.

"Be careful of him," the fortuneteller warned. "Zarka is a bad one!"

"We're not afraid of him," Jean replied.

"Zarka is a hothead," the fortuneteller said. "He will not take anyone's advice and stays away from camp for many hours. He will not say where he goes, and Zarka is making trouble for King Sando."

"You mean because of Nura?" Jean asked.

Sebenca nodded. "He demands the return of the money he paid for her."

"Why doesn't Sando give it back and call the whole thing off?"

"That is not so easy," Sebenca replied to Jean's question. "King Sando spent the money for a new trailer."

"That does complicate the situation," Jean admitted, frowning.

Louise had been thoughtful for several seconds.

On sudden impulse she asked the fortuneteller if she had a picture of Zarka.

"Why do you want it?"

"I have a hunch."

"Like a fortuneteller? You read the stars, perhaps?"

Louise laughed. "Nothing so glamorous as that. I'd like to show the picture to someone. If my hunch is correct, it may solve part of the mystery and will certainly help Nura."

"I have a snapshot of Zarka," Sebenca admitted. "It was taken a year ago at a gypsy wedding."

"May I borrow it?"

Sebenca hesitated a moment, then went to her van. Returning, she slipped it to Louise without any of the other gypsies seeing her action.

"For one gypsy to betray another is a crime," she muttered. "Zarka must never know that I gave it to you."

"He won't," Louise promised.

The girls left camp at once with Professor Crandall. Louise asked him to stop at the Penfield police station where she showed the photograph of Zarka to Chief Riley.

"Does this face look familiar?" she inquired.

The officer studied the photograph intently. Then

he called in a policeman named Staub. "Ever see this fellow before?" he asked.

"*H-m*," Staub said. "Except for the gypsy getup, he looks very much like the fellow I saw leaving that house we later found out was robbed. This is the same one, I'm sure."

"We'll pick him up for questioning," Chief Riley told his callers and thanked Louise for her quick thinking.

Upon reaching Starhurst School, Professor Crandall sought the girls' help in searching for his missing notes.

"Sebenca certainly gave me an idea!" he declared cheerfully. "I may find those papers in the cellar!"

Aided by Louise and Jean, he searched the basement for a full hour after dinner. Every old cabinet and discarded filing drawer was carefully examined. But the notes did not turn up.

"I might have known," the professor said despairingly. "It was foolish of me to place any faith in a fortuneteller."

"Don't give up yet," Jean said encouragingly.

The Danas had just returned to their room when Martha Frost came to tell Louise that she was wanted on the telephone.

"Maybe it's news about Nura!" Louise cried, starting for a second-floor extension.

The call was from Police Chief Riley, who reported

that Zarka had been identified and arrested at the gypsy camp.

"We have him in custody now," he announced. "So far, the man hasn't talked, but we think he will. There's no question but that he's guilty. Many thanks for your tip! We'll keep in touch with you."

Louise relayed the conversation to her sister, who was elated and said, "Now Zarka can't make any trouble for us or for Nura, either!"

She and Louise were just settling down to work on their class assignments when Doris Harland and Evelyn Starr tiptoed in. Since it was against the rules for any student to be out of her room at this hour, the Danas looked up in surprise.

"We're only going to stay a minute," Evelyn said, "but we have such exciting information we couldn't keep it."

Her eyes were dancing as well as Doris's.

"Tell us!" Jean demanded.

"It's about the mystery!" Evelyn told her excitedly. "Doris and I have turned up some evidence that will amaze you!"

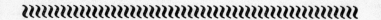

CHAPTER XXIII

Fire!

"TELL us what you learned! Please!" Jean urged the excited Doris and Evelyn. "New evidence, you say?"

"You and Louise will love this!" Evelyn laughed. "Wait until you hear what we've done!"

The Danas were puzzled. They had not found anything amusing in the gypsy mystery. In fact, it was quite the reverse. Yet their friends were laughing!

"Don't keep us in suspense!" Jean begged impatiently. "Is it about Professor Stanley?"

"Sort of." Doris nodded, and revealed that she and Evelyn had picked up their information at the drugstore in Penfield.

"The drugstore?"

"You know that soda-fountain boy whose name is Roy?"

"Yes."

181

"He told us that he wrote that mean note about you two girls being adopted from the gypsies and not being sisters."

"Roy!" Louise exclaimed in disbelief.

"Oh, he did it at the request of Lettie Briggs," Evelyn explained.

"So your guess was right," Jean said. "That girl ought to be taught a lesson!"

"We agree," said Evelyn emphatically, looking at Doris. Both girls chuckled mysteriously.

"But how does this have a connection with Professor Stanley?" Louise asked, perplexed.

"We're coming to that part," Evelyn replied. "And it's good! Doris and I induced Roy to write a note for us, signing it 'Your Favorite Professor.' It's a request for Lettie to meet him at the drugstore tomorrow at two o'clock."

The Danas laughed. "She'll get the letter in the Saturday morning mail?" Louise asked.

"Yes," said Evelyn. "I'll take a peek to be sure it's there."

"Lettie's so silly," Doris added, "she will be sure to think the message is from Professor Stanley."

"And trot downtown only to find he hasn't met her!" Evelyn chuckled. "Maybe it was a mean trick, but Lettie should be repaid for the cruel stunt she pulled."

Jean grinned. "I'd like to be in Penfield to see her reaction when Professor Stanley doesn't show up."

"Let's all go," Doris proposed. "We have to play in the tennis tournament at three, but we'll be back in plenty of time."

"I have another idea!" Jean said, tucking her feet up under her, Indian style. "How about asking Professor Crandall to go with us? He's a good sport and will enjoy the joke. I understand that he was very upset about the false story that Louise and I were gypsies."

"He can pretend to be Lettie's favorite professor!" Doris laughed. "Oh, I can't wait!"

First thing the next morning they sought out Professor Crandall. Though he protested mildly, the joke on Lettie appealed to his sense of humor and he finally agreed to accompany the girls. At ten minutes to two the professor and the four girls reached the drugstore and sat down in a rear booth. They ordered cokes and sipped them slowly. Two o'clock came and passed. Lettie did not arrive and an amused expression crossed Professor Crandall's face.

"Maybe she didn't get permission to come into town," Doris remarked anxiously. "That would be a joke on us!"

The professor chuckled. "Indeed it would."

"Don't give up yet," Louise said, seeing the look

of dismay on Doris's face. "Lettie usually is late for every appointment."

Jean gave her sister a quick nudge. "*Sh!*" she warned. "Here she comes now!"

Lettie, dressed in a tight-fitting black silk dress which made her look years older than she was, strolled into the drugstore. Fortunately, she did not see the group in the rear booth and went to the counter.

"Roy," Lettie asked in a dramatic tone, "has Professor Stanley been here yet?"

"Haven't seen him," the boy answered, suppressing a smile.

"I'm expecting him. He wrote me for a date."

Roy dived under the counter to hide the grin on his face.

Lettie sat down to wait near the door. She ordered ice cream and took a long while to eat it. At frequent intervals she glanced at her watch. Several times she arose and went to the store window to look up and down the street.

Several people came in, made purchases, and left. Lettie sighed audibly from time to time.

Those in the booth thoroughly enjoyed her impatience. But time was passing. The Danas and their friends would soon have to leave for their tennis match. The joke would have to be brought to a climax!

At a wink from Jean, Professor Crandall got up to play his part in the little drama. He sauntered over to Lettie's table.

"Good afternoon," he beamed. "Waiting for someone?"

"A friend," Lettie returned, looking none too pleased to have him sit down beside her.

Evelyn, Doris, and the Danas had come up from the rear of the store.

"Why, hello, Lettie!" Jean greeted her. "Enjoying the company of your favorite professor, I see!"

"My favorite professor—" Lettie echoed indignantly. She flushed and became confused.

Doris could not restrain a giggle. Lettie shot a suspicious glance at her, then saw that the others, even Professor Crandall, was smiling. Suddenly she realized that a joke had been played on her.

"Why, of all the mean things to do!" she cried.

"One good turn deserves another," Doris said.

Lettie launched into a long tirade. All the girls but Jean listened in amusement. Her eyes had become fixed on a car parked directly across the street.

Two men were entering it. As the automobile pulled from the curb, Jean was almost certain that one of the men was Professor Stanley!

"But he surely has changed," she said to herself.

The man no longer had a mustache and his hair was

now blond. Jean noted, however, that his features were the same as the fake professor's, and he had the familiar way of restlessly moving his hands.

The moment that the girls and Professor Crandall were outside the drugstore, having left Lettie still fuming, Jean mentioned her suspicions to the others.

"You're positive it was Professor Stanley?" Louise asked in amazement.

"Yes!"

"Which way did the car go?"

"Down Main Street in the direction of the cross-roads," Jean replied. "Professor Crandall, let's chase it."

"No, indeed," he said firmly. "I must get back to the school and you girls have a tennis match."

"But this is so important!" Jean urged.

"Then let the police handle it. We'll stop at head-quarters on the way home."

This was as much as the Danas could persuade him to do. Chief Riley thanked them for the tip and said he would pass the word on to the state police.

It was nearly three o'clock when the group reached Starhurst. The girls quickly changed their clothes and hurried to the tennis courts. There were many players, as this was the beginning of an interclass tournament.

The competition was keen, but in the end all four girls came out victorious. They were still in the tournament and would play the following Monday.

As the Danas were dressing for dinner, Louise decided to telephone Chief Riley and find out if Professor Stanley had been caught.

"Not a sign of him anywhere," was the report. "Nobody hiding at the Crossroads Inn, either."

Louise hung up the telephone and joined her sister on the stairway.

"No word yet," she announced. "But I can't get it out of my mind that he is hiding *somewhere* near the crossroads. It would explain the theft of food from King Sando's camp."

"You're right, Louise. But if Stanley's at the inn, he's clever enough to keep out of the way of the police."

"Jean," said Louise suddenly, "I wonder if Mrs. Crandall would let us go out to the gypsy camp tonight and see if Nura is there."

"I doubt it, but let's try."

After dinner the Danas went to the headmistress and asked permission to do a little questioning at the gypsy camp.

"You want to go there tonight!" Mrs. Crandall gasped in astonishment.

"We want to help Nura and Stivo," Jean urged.

"It would be unsafe indeed for you to go," the headmistress objected vigorously.

"The gypsies are our friends now," Louise pointed out. "They won't harm us."

"I'm not thinking of that. It's the woods and the mysterious old inn."

"We'll stay away from it," Jean promised. "And if we had an escort—"

"Have you someone in mind?" Mrs. Crandall asked. "Professor Crandall—"

"My husband is not too strong. In an emergency, you would need a younger, more able-bodied guard."

"How about Gus?" Louise suggested. He was the school's husky daytime guard. "With both Professor Crandall and Gus, we'd be well protected."

The headmistress was still very much against the proposed trip. Louise and Jean presented their case so well, however, that after consulting with her husband and Gus she finally gave her consent.

"Do use extreme caution," she advised the girls. "If anything should happen, I'd never forgive myself for having allowed you to make the trip."

"We'll be very careful," Louise promised.

Shortly after dinner the two girls and their escorts drove to the crossroads. The night was clear with a full moon rising over the treetops.

"I smell smoke," Jean announced as the station wagon pulled up at the crossroads.

"It's probably from the gypsy camp," responded Professor Crandall. "Another ceremonial, perhaps."

Leaving the parked vehicle, the four started off through the woods, carrying flashlights. There was a chill in the air. Jean, who led the way, buttoned her jacket about her throat.

"I still smell smoke," she remarked. "It's growing stronger, too."

They walked for several minutes, finally coming to the forked maple tree where they took the trail to the left that led to the camp. Now there was no question about the smoke.

"The gypsies must have a huge bonfire," Professor Crandall remarked.

As they rounded the last bend in the trail, the visitors stopped short, aghast at the sight ahead. Crimson tongues of flame were visible through the dark foliage. The next instant, they became aware of shouting and screaming.

"The gypsy camp is on fire!" Jean cried.

CHAPTER XXIV

Prisoners

AT THE gypsy camp everything was in a state of wild confusion. As Louise and Jean ran from the woods with Professor Crandall and Gus, they were dismayed to see flames surrounding the vans and tents on three sides. Some were on fire, as well as the grass and several trees.

Already the frantic gypsies had given up trying to battle the flames. Their one thought was to leave and take as many of their possessions as they could. Tents were being loaded into trucks and trailers.

Amid the barking of dogs and the screams of frightened children, men were shouting directions. King Sando alone seemed to retain his composure. He was overseeing the rounding up of the vehicles and trying to bring some semblance of order to the departure.

"The fire has too big a start for us to do much

good," Louise gasped. "Oh, these poor people."

"We must notify the fire department!" Gus cried.

"Yes," said Professor Crandall. "Come! There is no time to lose."

Louise and Jean wanted to stay, but he insisted that they get away from the inferno. The girls quickly scanned the milling throng of gypsies for a glimpse of Sebenca. They could not even see her van.

"Come quickly!" Professor Crandall urged the Danas.

The four hurried back to the station wagon and drove rapidly to a farmhouse to use a telephone. Louise, who made the call, said that they would wait there and direct the firemen to the gypsy camp.

When the engines raced up fifteen minutes later, Professor Crandall drove to a point from which it would be easiest to carry in the firefighting equipment.

Louise and Jean, concerned for the gypsies, raced on ahead toward the camp site. To their amazement every truck, trailer, and van had pulled out. There was no sign of anyone.

"I'm glad that they all got away safely," Louise said.

By this time, the fire had spread considerably. Tongues of flame rose in the dark sky to silhouette the bleak scene. Sparks dropping into piles of dead leaves started new fires.

A single unburned tent had been abandoned by

the gypsies. As the girls watched from a safe distance, a brand dropped on the dry canvas. In an instant the tent was ablaze.

The firemen went to work with chemicals and digging implements, quickly isolating the various blazes.

"I wonder how the fire started," Louise remarked to a supervising captain.

"It was set deliberately," he answered. "With gasoline. Not one fire, either, but a series of them."

"Not by the gypsies, certainly!" Louise exclaimed.

"Probably not," the captain agreed. "They were lucky to get out of here without losing all their equipment. Someone may have set the fires, hoping to run the gypsies out."

As he moved off, the sisters looked at each other. Who particularly would want to "run the gypsies out"?

"Louise," said Jean, "it's just possible that the person who set the fires is watching the result of his work. What say we scout around a bit and see if we can find anyone?"

"Yes, let's."

Moving from tree to tree the girls looked in every direction for the culprit. Several times flickering shadows deceived them, yet made their hearts beat excitedly.

By this time, the girls were near the Crossroads Inn.

The light from the fire was dim there. Jean was just about to turn on the flashlight she carried when the girls heard someone crashing through the woods.

"Maybe this is the person we're looking for!" Louise whispered. "When he gets closer, turn the light on him, Jean."

The sisters stood motionless and waited. As they listened, the Danas realized that not one but two persons were coming.

"They seem to know these woods well, even in the darkness," Jean murmured in Louise's ear.

A moment later she flashed the light directly in the oncomers' faces.

"Nura!" she exclaimed unbelievingly. There was a young man with her.

The gypsy girl, startled, cried out in Romany. With the light in her eyes she could not see who had spoken.

"We're the Danas," Louise explained quickly, and Jean beamed the flash on herself and her sister.

"Oh!" exclaimed Nura. "I am so glad to see you. Now I can thank you for all you've done for me. Such wonderful friends." Then, as a new thought struck her, she said, "How do you happen to be in the woods at this time of night?"

"We came to find out whether you were back," Louise answered.

Nura said that she had appeared at the old gypsy

camp a short while before. The messenger who had been assigned by Sebenca to watch for her had delivered the good news and they had started for King Sando's encampment at once.

"Nura, I'm sorry to have to tell you, but your enemies are still working against you," Louise said. "Someone tried to burn down the camp this evening."

"What!"

"Fortunately, everyone escaped and the fire is under control."

"I must see my father and mother at once!" the impetuous gypsy girl cried, starting off. "I must help them."

Louise put a restraining hand on Nura's arm. "Your people have vanished again," she said.

"My people have gone?" Nura exclaimed. "I must trail them. But first, I want to go to Stivo!"

"You know then that he still wants to marry you?" Louise asked. "Sebenca sent that message to you?"

"Yes. Oh, I am so happy. But sad, too, about the fire. I hope the tribe did not lose much."

"I don't believe they did," Louise told her kindly and added, "You'll be glad to hear that your father has consented to the marriage. On one condition, though. The skafidi must be recovered and Stivo's name cleared."

"Stivo is not a thief!"

"We'll find some way to prove that," Jean promised. "Louise and I think an impostor who calls himself Professor Stanley is involved in the thefts. We also suspect that he has been using the old inn and might even have hidden the stolen articles there. But we haven't been able to find them and neither have the police."

"Nura," Louise said suddenly, "did you ever come across any secret rooms in the inn?"

"Many," the gypsy girl replied.

"Oh, please show them to us," Jean begged. "We may be on the verge of solving the mystery of the stolen silver tray!"

First, Nura sent the messenger to the scene of the fire to try to pick up a clue on the whereabouts of her tribe.

"And please tell Professor Crandall we'll meet him and Gus at the station wagon," Louise added.

The young man hurried off and the girls sped to the old hotel. Entering the now familiar window, the Danas waited for Nura to lead the way.

"Have you seen the stone storeroom behind the pantry shelves?" she asked.

"No, Nura. Let's investigate it."

"Follow me," the gypsy girl said, taking the flashlight from Jean.

Sure of foot, Nura took the Danas to a room which evidently had served as a kitchen. Adjoining it was a small pantry with built-in shelves along the far wall. Nura pushed firmly against one end of the middle shelf. Slowly, the whole wall revolved.

The gypsy stopped it at the halfway point and the girls slipped through, noting that the wall had shelves on both sides. They pushed it back in place.

"Anything on these shelves?" Louise asked, directing the beam of her light on them.

"Only some old papers on the bottom one," Nura replied.

"Papers?" Jean demanded alertly.

She groped on the shelf to pick up a stack of them. Nura flashed the light so that Jean could read what she had found.

"These are Professor Crandall's missing notes!" she exclaimed.

"What a place to find them!" Louise cried, dumfounded. "How did they get here? He certainly never brought them."

"Someone else hid them here," Jean asserted, folding the notes and tucking them into her pockets. "That phony Professor Stanley, I'll bet! He's the one person who could use them."

"Do you know of any other hiding places, Nura?" Louise asked eagerly.

The gypsy girl hesitated. "There's another room underneath this one," she told them finally. "Do you want to go down there?"

"We don't especially want to, but we should," Louise said, laughing a bit uneasily. "Let's make a quick job of it."

Descending through a trap door, Nura showed the girls a loose stone in one of the walls.

"Nothing was hidden here before," she said, pulling out the stone. "I have looked." As a matter of routine, however, she flashed the light into the small recess. "There's something here now!" she cried.

Reaching in, Nura pulled out a small wooden box. She lifted the lid, and the girls gasped. The box was crammed with jewelry!

"From the Franklyn jewelry store, I'll bet!" Jean exclaimed. "What a discovery!"

By this time, the girls were so excited that they no longer gave any thought to personal danger. Louise took the box of jewels, then she and Jean asked Nura where the other secret rooms were located.

"We come now to a long, narrow passageway," the gypsy revealed, as the beam from the flashlight bobbed eerily up and down.

"Here is the entrance to another hidden room," she said presently.

The girls could see nothing and watched in fascination as Nura opened a heavy wooden panel that was cleverly painted to blend with the surrounding stonework.

Passing through this, the three groped their way

along to an inner door of thinner wood. Beyond, the passageway came to a dead end. As Nura played the flashlight beam over the walls, Jean spied a high shelf in the stonework. On it were a number of items wrapped in newspapers.

She pulled them down and set the parcels on the floor. Inside the first one was a paper bag. From it tumbled a handful of silver spoons. All were of the same pattern as the one which Jean had found many days earlier near the inn.

"Don't touch those!" Louise warned. "They may be poisoned."

"These spoons can't be old and rare," Jean reasoned. "There are too many of them. My guess is they're fakes, and not poisoned, either."

"That may be, but don't take chances," her sister begged.

"I won't," Jean said, carefully avoiding any contact with the silver.

Nura, meanwhile, had opened another of the packages. She uttered a shrill cry as a silver dish and a bracelet came to view.

"These belong to my tribe!" she cried. "They're some of the stolen articles!"

The last package, largest of all, remained unopened. Eagerly Louise removed the wrappings. Inside was a handsome silver tray with ornamental handles.

"The skafidi!" Nura exclaimed excitedly.

Louise and Jean were thrilled. "Now King Sando will approve your marriage to Stivo!" Louise laughed. "What a happy ending to the mystery!"

Nura, almost beside herself with joy, swung into a gay, whirling dance. Then, seizing Louise and Jean in turn, she gave them a kiss on each cheek. They merrily returned the show of affection. Finally Louise said:

"We must take these things away from here quickly."

Gathering up the skafidi and other treasures, the three girls started for the door. But as they reached it, the door slammed shut.

From beyond it came a sardonic laugh. A small panel in the door shot open. Professor Stanley's leering face appeared in the square opening.

"Good evening to you clever sisters," he greeted the Danas mockingly. "And this is Nura, the little gypsy who ran away?" When the girls did not answer, he added, "Planning to take my packages somewhere?"

The three girls were still too stunned to make any reply.

"Sorry, but I must keep you here," the fake professor went on. He locked the door. "It would never do for you to carry tales about me back to Starhurst and the police."

"You're an impostor!" Louise finally burst out.

"Those are harsh words, but I admit them," he said in a gloating manner.

"You tricked Mrs. Crandall into believing you were from a lecture bureau," Jean accused him.

"Mrs. Crandall is not a very discerning woman," he sneered.

"Your real name is Mixail Nikola!" Jean went on, determined to get at the truth. Hearing this, Nura gave a start and said that she had heard the name before.

"So you know?" the man replied with a harsh laugh. "Well, your knowledge will be of no use to you now!"

"It was you who started the fires tonight—to chase the gypsies away," Louise took up the accusation. "Why?"

"Since you'll never be able to carry tales, I don't mind answering your questions. The camp was too close to the inn. Convenient as it was for me to obtain food, it annoyed me to have so many people roaming around."

"You were afraid," Nura spoke up, "that my people would discover these stolen articles."

"Perhaps." The man gave another unpleasant laugh. "Whatever my reasons were, they'll make little difference to you now."

"You have betrayed your own people!" Nura said scornfully, her eyes flashing. "How could even you do that?"

"I am only half Romany. I care nothing for gypsy people. I hate them!"

"I see that!" Nura retorted angrily. "When you stole things you made it appear that other gypsies were to blame—even my own Stivo! You are evil and wicked!"

The gypsy girl then began to speak rapidly in her own tongue. Her words were obviously a scathing denunciation, for Nikola's face became livid with rage as he replied vehemently in Romany. For several minutes there was a heated exchange of remarks.

"This Nikola is heartless," Nura murmured to her friends. "He belongs to a tribe which always is in trouble with the police. Nikola and his helpers have been manufacturing silver spoons to sell as antiques. He used an old one for a pattern."

"That must have been the spoon we picked up in the woods," Jean said.

"It was," Nikola admitted with a laugh. "I learned at Starhurst School that you had it."

"So you stole it back?"

"I did. That spoon since has been sold at a very nice figure."

"You are very shrewd!" Jean said icily. "I suppose you threw that blanket around me at Starhurst too and tried to drag me off."

"Not I," Nikola replied loftily. "My assistant."

"Do you mean Zarka?" Louise guessed.

"I have friends who serve me well," Nikola answered evasively. "You girls were too curious and needed to be taught a lesson."

"But you didn't frighten us into giving up the case," Jean declared. "Let us out of here."

Nikola laughed sardonically. "Not a chance. But before I leave you, is there anything else you'd like to know?"

"You've been hiding at the inn for a long while—even before you tried to pass yourself off at school as a professor, haven't you?" Louise asked.

He nodded.

"And it was you who tried to frighten us away from here with confusing screams and horn blowing?" Jean pursued the questioning. "You knocked out Louise—"

"With a well-aimed stone," Nikola broke in, leering.

"How did you manage to deceive Mrs. Crandall?"

"It was very easy. The letter she received from the lecture bureau was written on stationery I—er—obtained during an interview there under another name. I took the liberty of signing the director's name."

"You mean you forged it," Jean corrected him in a disgusted tone. "And those evenings your lectures were canceled, you were no doubt away stealing these things."

Nikola admitted this was so. He was obviously proud of his dishonest exploits, particularly his part in the Franklyn jewelry-store robbery. He readily confessed that it was he who had snatched Nura's kerchief from Jean and left it in the store as a plant.

"Your helper Zarka has been arrested," Louise informed him.

"Too bad," Nikola said. "He should have been careful, as I am, and not get caught." The half-gypsy paused and narrowed his piercing eyes. "That fellow is lazy and stupid. Without my guiding hand, he would have failed in his thefts to get the money which he offered King Sando for Nura's hand."

Coolly the man disclosed that he had been annoyed by the interference of the Dana girls in his schemes. To discourage their sleuthing, he had tried to frighten them away from the inn. Further, he had circulated exaggerated rumors of ghost occupants to keep others from investigating the old building.

Nikola went on to reveal how he had used Lettie Briggs both as a means of obtaining information from the Danas and of thwarting the sisters in learning anything about him.

"Such a stupid girl!" he commented. "She turned out to be too much of a busybody."

"You've certainly made a full confession," Louise said when Nikola brought his narrative to a halt.

"Only because I want you to know how completely you have failed—despite all your snooping," the man sneered. "You disrupted my plans. So—you will never leave this cellar again."

"A bit dramatic, aren't you?" Jean demanded, in as scoffing a voice as she could manage, trying to curb a rising fear.

"At least let Nura go," Louise said earnestly. "She had nothing to do with whatever Jean and I did to spoil your schemes."

"Nura led you to the treasure here," Nikola replied. "She will not go free, either."

The girls fully expected that their captor would immediately take away the silver and jewels from them. But instead of unlocking the door to their prison, he moved back.

"I'll return later to get what belongs to me," Nikola told them.

At first the three girls stared at each other, nonplused. Why would he delay at all in snatching the precious articles?

But when, with a harsh laugh, Nikola slammed the door panel shut, the answer flashed upon the prisoners with sickening clarity.

With every source of ventilation cut off in the small cellar, suffocation would shortly overtake them!

CHAPTER XXV

A Woodland Wedding

As Mixail Nikola's receding footsteps echoed on the stone stairs outside their cellar dungeon, the Danas and Nura looked at each other, dazed with horror. In a little while the oxygen in the stuffy room would be used up!

"We must get out!" Jean cried frantically, breaking the awful stillness.

The girls threw themselves against the inner door and hammered with their fists. Their efforts were futile.

"It's no use," Nura murmured, choking down a wave of panic. "We're trapped!"

"If only someone would come!" Louise said, trying to keep her voice hopeful.

"To think I led you into this awful place," Nura almost sobbed. "It is all my fault."

"That isn't so, Nura," Louise assured her. "Besides,"

she added, "there might be another opening some-where. This room might open into an old tunnel that comes out somewhere beyond the inn."

"That's right," said Jean, taking heart. "Remember Professor Crandall's theory that this place had been used by escaping slaves during the Civil War?"

"It's our only chance!" said Nura, starting to ex-amine the walls.

Inch by inch the girls went over each stone. Almost ready to admit defeat, they met at the east wall. Sud-denly Jean cried gleefully:

"Here it is! Another camouflaged door!"

It was painted like the other one and proved to be merely wedged into an opening. It took untold per-severance, with no tools but their fingers, to remove it. At last the door fell inward, revealing a passageway beyond.

"Oh, thank goodness!" Jean exclaimed.

Louise was reserving her opinion. She hoped that the far end of the tunnel had not been sealed up! She offered to go ahead alone with the flashlight to find out. But the others would not hear of it.

"We will put this door in place," Nura suggested. "If Nikola comes, let him think the spirits have carried us and his treasure away!"

The girls picked up the silver and jewelry, then stepped through the opening. They propped the door into place, each one secretly wondering if the phony

professor knew about it. If only they could escape
before he might return to see how his evil scheme
was working.

Groping their way along the dank passage, they
were suddenly dismayed to have the flashlight grow
dim. A moment later it winked off.

The three held hands and proceeded in the inky
blackness. Nura, sure-footed and used to traveling in
the dark, led the way. She guided the Danas with re-
markable skill.

"This passage seems endless!" Jean said ten minutes
later, and the others agreed.

After that the girls trudged on in silence, each trying to conceal her mounting fear. Then, suddenly,
Nura cried out:

"Oh! I see faint light ahead!"

"Where?" the Danas chorused excitedly, and the
next instant gasped in delight. Some distance away an
unmistakable crack of light broke the darkness.

"I smell fresh air, too!" Louise added thankfully.

In their excitement the girls almost ran now to the
end of the tunnel. Here the floor sloped rapidly up-
ward to the exit which was blocked by a huge boulder.

"Now if only we can get out!" Jean cried. "This
boulder must weigh a ton."

"You're right," Nura agreed. "I hope we can move
it before Nikola finds us."

Louise eyed the obstacle thoughtfully. "Perhaps if

we all push together, it'll move enough for us to squeeze by."

"Let's try," said Nura.

By exerting every ounce of their combined strength, the girls were able to move the big stone only a few inches.

"If only we had a lever of some sort!" Jean gasped, out of breath.

The girls felt around the floor of the passageway but could find nothing to help them.

"Let's try again!" Louise urged, bracing herself for a supreme effort. "We mustn't give up!"

Once again the three heaved together. This time the boulder moved several inches.

"I think I can squeeze through now!" Jean cried.

Taking a deep breath, she wriggled through the narrow opening, then helped pull out Louise and Nura. Gazing gratefully at the full moon, the girls drew the fresh night air deep into their lungs.

"I wonder where we are," Louise said a few seconds later, looking around at the unfamiliar surroundings.

Nura thought they must be some distance back of the inn, so the trio started off through the dense woods with their packages in search of the road.

After about ten minutes of fast walking they found it and presently came to the car. Professor Crandall and Gus were waiting! Laughing in sheer relief, the Danas climbed in and hugged the professor.

"Oh, we're so glad to see you!" Louise said. "We thought we'd never see you or anybody else again!"

"What's this? What's this?" the professor asked in bewilderment. "Where have you been?"

Both sisters took turns explaining their recent adventure. The men were flabbergasted when Jean described the encounter with the fake professor. They were astounded further when the girls showed them the lost notes, jewels, silver, and the skafidi.

"Incredible!" murmured the professor.

"We must get word to the police immediately," Professor Crandall urged. "If that impostor can be captured, the mystery will be completely solved!"

Nura climbed in and they hastened to state police headquarters. Captain Smith was overwhelming in his praise.

"May we use your telephone?" Louise asked.

"Go ahead, by all means."

She put in a call to Stivo at the Rose Tree Restaurant. When he answered, she said:

"This is Louise Dana. Someone here wants to speak to you." She turned the telephone over to Nura.

"Stivo!" was all the gypsy girl had to say, and he knew at once whose voice it was.

The conversation, entirely in Romany, was short but most affectionate, and an hour later at Starhurst School there followed a wonderful reunion for the gypsy couple. In addition, Louise and Jean were besieged by their friends and teachers, who showered them with praise and questions all at once. Mrs. Crandall was so relieved to see the girls unharmed that she did not reprimand them for the risks they had taken.

In the midst of the merriment and gay confusion, word came that Mixail Nikola had been captured by the state police. And Zarka had made a full confession. Money, jewelry, and silver would be returned to their rightful owners.

"With Zarka and Nikola in jail, your troubles will be over," Louise smilingly remarked to Nura.

"They are now," the gypsy agreed, her dark eyes shining. "Once my father has the skafidi, he will approve my marriage to Stivo. A gypsy never breaks a promise—or forgets the kindness of friends such as you."

To find the gypsies new camp was the only remaining problem. However, through gypsy messengers who had been dispatched by Sebenca, they learned that the new camp was located in a beautiful glen not far from Penfield. Joyfully Nura and Stivo went to rejoin their people, taking with them the tribal treasures recovered by the Danas at the Crossroads Inn.

"You will hear from us again," they assured Louise and Jean in departing. "God be with you until then."

Several days passed, but no word came. At Starhurst School, Louise and Jean kept wondering what had happened to Nura and Stivo. Had the gypsy camp left the Penfield area altogether? And what of the wedding? Had King Sando changed his mind again and refused to allow the couple to marry?

Just before lunch one day the Danas went to look for mail. As they approached their box in the lobby, a whining voice greeted them:

"You two surely made a big mistake turning over all that silver to the gypsies." It was Lettie Briggs.

The girl was annoyed that the sisters had solved a perplexing mystery. But even more, Lettie was extremely discomfited because her friend "Professor Stanley" had been exposed as a common thief and impostor.

"You'll never hear from that gypsy Nura again!" Lettie went on, with a haughty expression.

"Oh, no?" Louise said softly. "I'm glad to say you're wrong, Lettie."

She had just drawn a letter from the mailbox and was looking at the sender's name on the envelope.

"It's from Nura!" she said excitedly.

Ripping the envelope, the sisters eagerly scanned the message.

Nura wrote that she and Stivo were very happy—they were to be married the next day. The letter ended by inviting Louise, Jean, Miss Parker, and Professor Crandall to come to the gypsy camp for the wedding festivities.

Mrs. Crandall readily consented to the Danas' being away from classes the following day. Gaily they set off with the two teachers.

Never were Louise and Jean to forget the occasion! Gypsy tribes, in their most brilliant costumes and wearing glistening earrings and necklaces, had gathered from all sections of the countryside for the ceremony.

When Nura appeared, she looked radiant in her bright red wedding attire. Stivo, standing very erect, looked even more handsome than before. In front of the tribunal they spoke their marriage vows in Romany.

Stivo's right wrist then was joined with Nura's. A quick incision was made, permitting the blood of the two to mingle. The ceremony was complete.

"On with the music!" shouted King Sando.

Fiddlers played tirelessly for ceremonial dancing. Guests were served great quantities of roast chicken and pig, and exotic foods which the Danas had never tasted before.

Finally the girls were thinking of slipping away when abruptly the music ceased. A hush fell upon the throng.

King Sando and his queen Jiva came slowly toward Louise and Jean. In their hands they bore the fine silver skafidi which the sisters had recovered.

The girls assumed that they were witnessing another ceremony in connection with the wedding. To their surprise and embarrassment, the gypsy king halted directly in front of them.

"For you—our friends," he said simply. He extended the beautiful silver tray.

"Oh, no!" Jean protested. "We couldn't take such a valuable gift."

Sebenca whispered in her ear, "Take it! King Sando will be offended if you do not. You have returned his only daughter to him. All our people want you to have the skafidi."

Taking the old fortuneteller's advice, Louise and Jean graciously accepted it, thanking all the gypsies.

Professor Crandall turned to shake Sebenca's hand. "I have some thanks of my own to give," he remarked jovially. "Sebenca, your fortunetelling proved most prophetic. I found my notes—or rather, Louise and Jean did—under stones, as you said."

"So now you believe?" Sebenca smiled. "I am glad."

Both Professor Crandall and Miss Parker urged the wise old gypsy to tell the fortunes of Louise and Jean. This Sebenca willingly agreed to do.

Quickly she spread out the cards. With scarcely a glance at their markings, she smiled at the two girls.

"I see happiness ahead," she predicted. "Many wonderful years."

"What, no trouble?" Jean chuckled. "Not even a little?"

"Much trouble," Sebenca admitted. "Ah, yes, trouble, trouble, but you will meet it with courage as always. I see mystery too! And adventure! You will like that, and it will come to you."

How true this proved to be as Louise and Jean undertook to solve THE GHOST IN THE GALLERY.

"I bless you now, both of you," the fortuneteller went on, "and give you a gypsy good-by. A Romany welcome wherever you follow the long trail!"